Praise for *Angela Sloan*

"Angela Sloan is a winning fourteen-year-old heroine and way too honest to be an effective Watergate burglar. This smart, poignant, funny book almost makes me thankful for the Nixon presidency."
— Matthew Sharpe, author of *You Were Wrong* and *Jamestown*

"The teenage daughter of a former CIA agent, Sloan takes us on a wild ride as she confronts not only a crazy cast of characters but secrets of her own past—all the while maintaining her undercover identity . . . bold, edgy, and downright comic."
— Susan Gregg Gilmore, author of *The Improper Life of Bezellia Grove* and *Looking for Salvation at the Dairy Queen*

Praise for James Whorton, Jr.

"Whorton's deadpan comic genius exploits misunderstandings for laugh-out-loud results. A joy."
— *Kirkus*, starred review

"Fast paced, often hilarious, always readable . . . thoroughly exhilarating. To those who thought minimalism in fiction was moribund, think again; Whorton . . . gives it a fresh and revitalizing shot in the arm."
— Stephen Dixon, author of *I.*

"Whorton conjures through close observation a hilariously absurd world that holds, just possibly, the keys to its own salvation. Amid the absurdity, you can feel the hope."
— *The Tennessean*

"Whorton has created characters, who, amid conversations about engines and sex and amid beer-drinking bouts and efforts to dodge responsibility, seek answers to the fundamental questions about life and who often discover their better selves in the process."
— *Lexington Herald-Leader*

ALSO BY JAMES WHORTON, JR.

Frankland
Approximately Heaven

ANGELA SLOAN

A Novel

James Whorton, Jr.

FREE PRESS

New York London Toronto Sydney

Free Press
A Division of Simon & Schuster, Inc.
1230 Avenue of the Americas
New York, NY 10020

First Free Press trade paperback edition August 2011

FREE PRESS and colophon are trademarks of Simon & Schuster, Inc.

For information about special discounts for bulk purchases,
please contact Simon & Schuster Special Sales at
1-866-506-1949 or business@simonandschuster.com

The Simon & Schuster Speakers Bureau can bring authors to your live event. For more information or to book an event contact the Simon & Schuster Speakers Bureau at 1-866-248-3049 or visit our website at www.simonspeakers.com.

Designed by Carla Jayne Jones

Manufactured in the United States of America

10 9 8 7 6 5 4 3 2 1

Library of Congress Cataloging-in-Publication Data

ISBN 978-1-4516-2440-3
ISBN 978-1-4516-2441-0 (ebook)

To Nora

ANGELA SLOAN

Yellow Post Road
Wigmore, WV
December 19, 1972

Dear Central Intelligence Agency:

Your polygraph examiner, Mr. Jerry Wicker, has just now left my house. After questioning me for two hours in the voice of a sleepy robot, he has declared me "unreliable" and "unnatural." He calls me a "strange, dry girl."

For two hours I sat at the dining room table, wired to his aluminum suitcase, watching a brown felt sideburn curl away from his cheek. Glue failure! Now he accuses me of lying to him. My "flat eye line" and "suspicious hand carriage" have given the game away.

Let me say this about lying. When a person is fourteen years old and traveling on her own by car, she has got to have some stories in her pocket. Every trucker with a tremor in his arm wants to know where that girl's dad is. Even the clerk at the Lee-Hi Motor Hotel feels he is owed a piece of her life story, if only so he can repeat it when someone comes asking. So yes, I got into the habit of making things up. But the truth was always real to me. I never lied to make myself feel better.

Does somebody in Langley need to feel better?

That is not a good reason to lie.

Most people's fathers aren't perfect, and Ray Sloan is no exception. I don't expect you to defend him in the papers. I admit I didn't help matters any with my activities last summer when the FBI was looking for him. I was trying to lie low, but then I got involved in that other business with the terrorist hippies.

The fiasco at the Watergate was a surprise to me. It was a thing that Ray had really almost nothing to do with. Still, I will tell you what little I know about it, plus everything about the Chinese Communist girl known as Betty or Ding.

Please excuse my faulty typing. Having sat here these minutes beating this out, I have had the chance to remind myself that Mr. Wicker was only doing his job, perhaps to the best of his ability. I suppose he was following some important rule when he did not permit me to answer any of his questions beyond a yes or no. I thank you for your consideration in sending Mr. Wicker here, since driving to Langley for a lie detector test would have required me to miss a day of school. I have Mr. Wicker's rubber mole that he left on the edge of the sink.

Now I am going to tell you what really happened. The whole thing. No stories. In order for it all to make sense, I will have to back up first. I will keep it as short as I can.

Because of the truthful and explicit nature of what follows, please consider this a Top Secret Correspondence.

2

There are some things I can't explain about Ray. Why did he drink too much? I don't know. Why did he save my life at a moment when his own life had exhausted him?

He was not my father in the biological sense. Other people didn't know that, because it was our cover. Even with friends inside the Agency, there was no need to discuss such things. Why would there be? We didn't see a need, anyway. It is easier to live your cover if you live it all the time, day and night, in public and in private, and even when you're alone.

But I can remember my previous parents, of course. I was seven when they were murdered by Simbas outside Stanleyville, along with my small brother and our Congolese housekeeper, Judith. I survived the massacre by hiding myself in an orange tree, where I still was clinging like a bat when Ray arrived in a yellow beer truck and spied me among the branches. He was someone who'd visited our place once or twice—an acquaintance of my father's. He plucked me down. "*N'ayez pas peur,*" he told me in his Okie-inflected French. Don't be scared. He walked all over the muddy yard with me shaking in his arms.

This was the summer of 1964, when the Simba rebellion was happening in the Congo. Many white people had left Stanleyville, and those who hadn't left were stuck. Simbas controlled the airport and had overrun the U.S. Consulate. The consular staff, including some Agency men, were hostages. Ray worked under nonofficial cover, though, so he had no connection to the consulate. He was a manager with the Sheffield Beer Distributing Company. He hid me in a room at the Sheffield warehouse.

The Simbas, as I recall them, were a frightening mob of orphans high on cannabis and beer. They dressed in animal skins, ladies' wigs, and secondhand military clothing, and they armed themselves with spears and stolen rifles. Their witch doctors worked a kind of magic that was said to transform bullets into water. Soon a pack of these sad killers searched the warehouse and found me. One of them had lipstick on his eyelids. Perhaps you can imagine my terror after what I had seen them do to my family. But Ray was there in an instant. He told them I was a drowned girl who had come back to life, and if any man touched me his body would dry up like a husk. He sent the boys away with a truckload of Sheffield ale.

I remember those weeks at the warehouse in pieces. There was cha-cha music on the radio, in between the death sentences that were announced several times every day. Once I cut my hand while trying to open a can of sardines, and I shrieked my lungs out while Ray poured alcohol over the wound and wrapped it. "Easy, Jumbo," he said. Another time, I was sitting in the yard in some white sunlight when we heard trucks. Ray scooped me up off the ground and ran to put me inside. I felt both frightened and protected.

In November 1964, Belgian paratroopers retook Stanleyville. The Simba retreat was chaotic and bloody. The government in Leopoldville, unable to rely on its own army, had sent a column of white mercenaries to rescue all the Europeans and put them on planes. A pair of these mercenaries came to the warehouse, and Ray lifted me into the back of their truck. There was a nun back there with her ankle taped up. I thought Ray was coming in after me, but then he didn't. I screamed when the truck pulled away without him.

The nun began to sing "Amazing Grace." I don't quite remember assaulting her, but evidently I did. She was bitten in places where she could not have bitten herself. I guess I did it. They turned the truck around.

I jumped down from the truck and ran calling for Ray. There was an office in the warehouse and that was where I found him, playing a record on his portable phonograph and holding a long, skinny pistol on his knee. He appeared confused to see me again. Hadn't he just sent me away? Something was happening inside him that was too quiet for a seven-year-old girl to understand. I had interrupted something, but I could not guess what.

It didn't matter. I grabbed him, and this time I wasn't letting go.

The men with the truck had followed me in. "She will have to be hog-tied," one of them said.

"It's either that or leave her with you," the other one said to Ray. "And then you will *both* have your livers eaten."

I crawled up onto Ray's lap, sniveling into his neck, begging him to come with me.

Whatever Ray's plan had been—whatever it was he'd intended to do when the record finished playing—he set it aside. He took two passports from a locked drawer of the desk, and he carried me to the truck. This time he climbed in with me.

"I am sorry for my daughter's behavior," he said to the nun.

I can never express the gratitude and love I felt then and continue to feel.

"I have seen friends killed by children," the nun said, "but I hadn't expected to die at the hands of a *white* child."

"Her name is Angela," Ray said, and it has been ever since.

3

I was very lucky to have found Ray. Who else could have tolerated such a strange, dry girl with suspicious hand carriage and a flat eye line? Maybe I was normal once. I wonder. Anyway, I clearly wasn't normal anymore. Bad things had happened. I had tasted nun.

I stuck to Ray like a strap. He was a solid man, five-foot-eleven-and-a-half, with a face that was creased and tanned because he never wore a hat. His hands were dark and somewhat knobby. He had an exceedingly normal hand carriage—calm and steady. The nails of the first fingers of his right hand were yellow from nicotine. His eye line was straightforward. He could look at you for a long time without seeming to stare. He would just look at anything, watching.

We never went back to Stanleyville. The Sheffield Beer Distributing Company went on with another Agency man at the desk. Ray took me with him to Camp Peary, or "the Farm," where he became a highly valued instructor.

I loved the Farm. I attended boarding school in Williamsburg, but I would have stayed at the Farm year-round if I could have, feeding the feral cats behind the cafeteria and observing the Venus flytraps in the swamp by the overflow parking lot. It was an excellent environment for me.

I was considered by all to be Ray's daughter. I still had the old passport that Ray had brought from his desk at the warehouse, which described me as an American born in the Congo. The passport bore the photo of a nondescript white baby. It must have occurred to me many times, I am sure, to wonder who she was. Of course I wondered about her. But I never brought it up with Ray. Why delve into something like that?

Breaks from school were spent at the Farm, where I learned to keep out of the way. When I try, I'm pretty good at not being noticed.

I can sit on the edge of a stool like a gargoyle for one hour, and people don't seem to see me. It helps if you are a little bit homely.

And yet I did manage to make a few friends at the Farm. The women in the cafeteria will remember me, and Miss Evans let me use the library in return for helping her out with shelving books and so on. Not that she needed much help. She gets by very well with one arm. I passed long afternoons in a soft chair in her office, reading about the Berlin tunnel, the Jedburgh teams who jumped from planes into occupied France, and many less famous exploits of the old OSS. History was my preferred subject, though I can read just about anything as long as it has a clear prose style and a basis in reality. For example, the novel *Black Beauty* by Anna Sewell has a wealth of information about horse care in it. That one was not a part of the Farm library. Miss Evans brought it to me from her home shelf.

In January of 1972, a distinguished career came to its end when Raymond W. Sloan retired from the Central Intelligence Agency. We said goodbye to the Farm and to the town of Williamsburg, where I had ridden along with Ray on many surveillance and surveillance detection drills. We moved to D.C. and took a furnished rental on I Street in the Foggy Bottom neighborhood. The landlady was a widow named Edel. She lived next door. Often she would pop in with a dish of spaghetti or salmon croquettes, lingering to see us eat or to give me a lesson on the Chickering piano that took up most of the front room, along with an antique sofa that was covered in scratchy maroon velvet. At the window there was a sprawling, long-trunked dieffenbachia plant.

Those are some of the details of our life. I enrolled in public school and attended, mostly. I can't say that I loved my ninth-grade experience in Washington, D.C. One day smoke came out of the ceiling and we all ran down the hall. That was one of the better days.

Ray took long walks, and in homeroom I kept my sunflower knapsack on a counter by the window so that he would know which room I was in, should he happen to pass. I saw him go by once or twice. Because of an old injury, Ray kicked his left leg a little high and to the side when he walked. You could notice it more from a distance than up close.

Let me tell about Ray some more. He was a gentle-natured man who almost never raised his voice. I can only think of one time when he did it. He usually wore a permanent-press shirt with a light blue windbreaker jacket, tan poplin slacks, and hard shoes with a polish. He grew up in Oklahoma, and though he'd worked hard to have no accent, he still said "maysure" instead of "measure." I don't think he heard the difference. He passed on to me his values of toughness, stoicism, and keeping a low overhead. He also showed me something about the practice of a craft.

In our new life in D.C., one thing we both missed badly was the Farm cafeteria. We ate at the Peoples Drug Store or a couple other places that had the kind of food we liked. At night Ray settled in at the kitchen table. We kept the television there, since Mrs. Edel forbade smoking in the room where her couch, piano, and draperies were. He'd have a drink while we watched the news together, and after I went upstairs he'd have many more. I knew he drank too much. I never kept track of bottles, but he'd go through several trays of ice each night. Sometimes I'd hear him getting sick. However, the thing about "too much" is this: how much too much is too much? A person can eat too much every day of his life and still die old. Some people talk too much yet never pay a price for it. Some people think too much. For Ray and me, I saw no reason why things could not go on as they were.

Upstairs I had a bedroom of my own. That was a welcome change from boarding school. It was quite a luxury to get up there and sit at my desk without a half dozen inquisitive girls on every side of me. I would read *The Scarlet Letter* or construct a polygon in my notebook using a compass and a straightedge. As much as I disliked ninth grade, I did my homework conscientiously, not wanting to screw things up and find myself back in boarding school. Ray needed me with him, and with him was where I wanted to stay.

4

One bad habit that I did have was that I sometimes slipped out of school early. But on Wednesday, May third, I stayed to the bell. I walked home and found Ray in the kitchen with his head on the table. He sat up abruptly, blinking.

"Where have you been?" he said.

I told him about staying to the bell.

"Good move, Jumbo," he said. He snapped his fingers. "I'm also trying to better myself today."

"How?"

He wouldn't say, but later I found a half-full pint of bourbon in the kitchen wastebasket.

We watched some of *Let's Make a Deal,* and then we played Scrabble with an old set of Mrs. Edel's that was in a brown box. Ray's hand twitched, brushing some tiles onto the floor.

"Are you out of cigarettes?" I said.

"Yes. But I don't have to rush out the moment the cigarettes are gone."

"Okay."

His knee was bobbing, and he was squinting at the ceiling.

"Let's go get some cigarettes," I said.

He popped out of his chair and hit the front steps at a jog. We crossed Virginia Avenue, and Ray got two orange and gold packs of Raleighs at the grocery under the Watergate. He lit a cigarette in the plaza.

There is a sharp smell that issues from a newly lit cigarette which I have always enjoyed. I don't know why it smells different at first. Ray grimaced as he drew the smoke in, and a change came over him. The edginess lifted away. He smiled at his mistake. "I shouldn't try to do two things at once," he said.

He meant giving up the two habits. He was right, I thought.

I was holding a bag with two cans of SpaghettiO's in it, but we decided not to dirty up the kitchen. We crossed Virginia Avenue again and had taken our usual booth at the Howard Johnson's when a man came in, a person of medium height or a little less, dressed in a business suit. I had not seen him before. He sat at the counter, and I saw him peering around the restaurant, scrutinizing faces. The waitress pulled a chrome knob to fill a glass with milk for him. Because we were regulars there I can tell you the waitress's name: Audrey. Any of these details can easily be checked with her.

The man in the suit stared at Ray for a long while. Finally Ray gave him a tiny nod. This was the man we would later refer to as HORSEFLY.

HORSEFLY approached our table and requested in a loud voice to borrow some butter pats. Quietly he added, "Watch me, Ray." He went away into the men's room and came out with a sore grin on his mouth. He limped past our table with his head stuck down. The collar of his shirt stood away from the crinkly white backside of his neck.

He made a loop in the Howard Johnson's dining room. His limp had a store-bought look to it. It seemed fake and self-inflicted.

"See how I'm walking," he hissed when he passed close to us again.

We ate our meal. For Ray, it was chicken salad and soup. For me, a hamburger with mayonnaise. The man lingered over his milk until some customers had left, and then he sat beside me on the booth seat. "I am wearing a gait-altering device which I donned just now in the men's room," he said.

"No kidding," Ray said.

"It's in my shoe. It came from *the place*. You know what place I'm talking about." HORSEFLY swept his gaze across the restaurant again.

I ought to have mentioned his age before now. He was Ray's age, late fifties. Another retired Agency man.

I pretended to be absorbed in a connect-the-dots puzzle on the back of the paper place mat. HORSEFLY advised Ray that he was setting up a small shop in town for the purpose of handling sensitive domestic matters. "I need a man with operational experience and a boatload of discretion. Someone like yourself. What do you say?"

"Thanks, but I've retired," Ray said.

In my mind I approved of that answer. There was something I didn't like about this man.

HORSEFLY looked at me and nodded hello, as though he had just now noticed that yellow-haired gargoyle on the far end of the booth seat. He wrote out a number on the corner of my place mat and tore it off. "If you change your mind, you can reach me on my secure phone at the *Ite-whay Ouse-hay*. You heard me right."

HORSEFLY limped back to the men's room to remove his painful gait-altering device. Later without a glance at us he glided out the door.

5

Ray pushed the scrap of paper into his windbreaker pocket. He scarcely blinked as he smoked one cigarette, then another down to the filter. We walked home under a drizzle.

In the kitchen Ray cracked a tray of ice on the counter and asked me to put the Scrabble set away. When I came back he was standing in front of the television with the cold bottom edge of a glass of bourbon pressed against his eyelid. He'd sent me out of the room so I wouldn't see him take the bottle out of the wastebasket.

I went upstairs. The bedroom I used had been decorated by Mrs. Edel for her twin granddaughters. There were twin wrought-iron beds, twin vanities with flip-up mirrors in them—twin everything. All the furniture was painted in ivory and gold, and the bunched-up white drapes matched the bed ruffles. I sat up there like an insect in a jar of cotton balls. I attempted to read *The Scarlet Letter*.

At some point I discovered my mouth had been hanging open so long that the inner walls of my cheeks were dry. I was thinking about HORSEFLY. I set the book down and examined my hands, front and back. I had a cut on one of my knuckles where I had knocked it on the edge of a bulletin board. I flipped up a vanity mirror to have a look at my own face, and I noticed for the seventh time that my eyebrows were too heavy. My nose was rudimentary, somehow, like the nose on a face card.

I raised the window and drew in a long breath from the rain-splattered alley. At the Farm when it was wet like this you would sometimes come across mobs of frogs, I mean hundreds of them, tangled together and struggling with their slippery legs.

My thoughts were here and there until I heard the rip of the weather-stripping on the alley door below. Whenever that door opened it sounded like splitting wood. Then it shut, and I heard the smack of shoe leather against the wet pavement in the alley.

6

In the morning I found Ray at the kitchen table asleep with his head on his arms, still dressed in his clothes from the night before. The salt-and-pepper hair was ropy on top of his head. He'd been rained on.

I emptied the beanbag ashtray and started some coffee. The percolator gave a slurp, and Ray sat up with a line in his cheek from his jacket cuff. He rinsed his eyes at the sink.

"Let's forget I wasn't here last night," he said.

"All right."

I led him to the scratchy velvet sofa in the front room, and he stretched out with his ankles on the armrest. I got his shoes off. I went to school.

School that day was a special chore. I worried about Ray, and Mr. Tinker's Henny Youngman routine in Ancient Civilization was hard to sit through. To distract myself, I was taking my pen apart and putting it back together. Tinker's allergies gave him sneezing fits, only he didn't like to sneeze in front of the class, so he stifled his sneezes. "Tink! Tink!" That's the sound his sneezes made, trying to erupt.

When I felt I'd had enough, I went to the front of the room and told Mr. Tinker I needed to see the nurse. "I don't feel so good," I explained.

"Nobody does."

"I may throw up," I said. I purposely let some dribble show at the corner of my mouth.

Tinker wrote me out a pass.

I didn't go to the nurse's office but slipped into the empty lunchroom. The floor was wet from mopping, and my sandal soles left milky tracks. No matter. Outside, the janitor sat on a school chair from which the backrest had been sawed off. He was having a smoke. He stepped himself around in a half circle to show me his back.

It was a quick trot from my school to the alley behind I Street. I found Ray at our kitchen table, working the *World News Digest* crossword. He was in a talking mood.

"You must have gathered that I have come unretired. You know what that means. There will be some nights out. We'll also need code words for persons we might refer to. Look here." We chose cryptonyms at random from the crossword answers.

We decided to eat in that night. I drained a can of artichokes and combined them in a glass bowl with half a small jar of mayonnaise and a quarter spoonful of celery salt. I baked it, and then we ate it with Captain's Wafers. After that we went out for cigarettes and wound up walking all the way to the Tidal Basin, where the cherry trees seemed to have thrown off their blossoms all at once, fluffing the surface of the water near the shore. It was pretty out.

When we got home Ray polished our shoes. In spite of my worries, it was good to see him unretired.

7

Of the business itself, leading up to the Watergate break-in, I didn't observe much. What I did see only confirmed my poor first impression of HORSEFLY.

The next time I saw him was a Saturday, the sixth of May. Ray and I took a cab to Georgetown, where we did some sidewalk technique. Here I am referring to ways for a person on foot to discover whether he is being followed. It was a practice Ray had taught at the Farm, and I knew something about it myself, having gone along with him often for those exercises in Williamsburg, Newport News, and Richmond. When we knew we were clean, we had a second cab drop us alongside a bright, squirming clot of hippies at Dupont Circle.

A crowd of hippies is a centerless thing. A number of them were facing a girl who stood on a bench declaiming, but I saw they weren't listening, only waiting in line for corn on the cob. The girl was preaching over their heads. She was dressed like Hiawatha except for the green water pistol in her belt.

We circled the park until we encountered HORSEFLY and another man to whom we afterward referred by the cryptonym GRISTLE. Both were dressed all in white as though just off the tennis court. GRISTLE was a former FBI man with a stiff black mustache.

"I see you brought your girl," HORSEFLY said.

GRISTLE looked me up and down several times. "I won't mind having her along," he said. "That way we don't seem to be *casing the joint.*"

We walked along Massachusetts Avenue. GRISTLE gargled out the orders. "Appear to be tourists! View every detail. Look here, this fence post has a tiger head on it. Let's all stand here viewing this tiger head." His long, theatrical laugh startled me. HORSEFLY fell in with a ga-ga-ga kind of sound. Ray shaded his eyes.

We stopped again in front of a certain embassy. If you're reading this, you'll know which one.

"We will never get in through the front," HORSEFLY said.

GRISTLE told me to run off down a side street. "Pretend you are chasing a puppy."

"There is no puppy," I said.

"Pretend you saw a duck."

I did what he asked. First I called out, "A duck!" Then I ran off down the side street and into the alley behind the embassy building.

GRISTLE came after me alone.

"The duck got away," I said.

He directed me to tie my shoes. I was wearing my sandals, but I took one off and shook some imaginary gravel out of it. GRISTLE wasn't done inspecting the building, so I did the other sandal, too. I followed him back to where the others were, and the four of us walked on.

"There is a service entrance with an alarm system," GRISTLE said. "I will need to shoot out the streetlights."

"We go in one week from today," HORSEFLY said.

He and GRISTLE got into a cab and were gone.

Ray shook his head. Their tradecraft was embarrassing. I hesitate to even call it tradecraft. Ray and I didn't discuss it, however. We took a cab, a walk, and another cab home to I Street.

Ray was gone all of the following weekend. He came home early Monday morning, the fifteenth of May. A person can draw his own conclusions. If you read the *Post* that afternoon, you saw that there'd been a burglary at the Chilean Embassy on Massachusetts Avenue. What HORSEFLY could have wanted from there, I don't know. The paper said a couple of radios were missing and some drawers had been gone through. It looked to be the work of petty thieves.

8

Also on that Monday, George Wallace was shot. I will give you what I have on that, though you'll know most of it already if you have talked to Mrs. Edel.

Having the landlady next door is not an arrangement I would recommend to anyone involved in clandestine operations. She was an observer, and she liked to pop in when Ray was away on his "business trips." She asked whether it did not frighten me to be in the house alone. Really she was talking about herself, I guess. "People don't know what work it is to go the whole day with no conversation," she said. "You must knock on my door anytime you want company."

"I'll do that," I promised.

On the Monday I'm referring to, she popped in around nine in the morning. Ray had been gone all weekend, as I said, and I'd stayed home from school to wait for him. To pass time I'd been drawing a floor plan on a sheet of graph paper. I showed it to Mrs. Edel. The plan was for a fanciful kind of house with a barn connected to it. Horses could enter the living room to munch hay or simply stand there, as they wished.

"How delightful," Mrs. Edel said. "You should call your creation 'Hoof House.'"

I wrote it along the bottom of the sheet.

Mrs. Edel pointed out that I was not at school. I asked her to give me a piano lesson. She was leading me through some scales when Ray came in.

His forehead was like wet plaster, and his hair stuck out as though he had slept against a car seat. He had a fresh cigarette on his lip, not burning.

"Good morning to you," he said to Mrs. Edel. He lunged past us into the kitchen. I heard him crack an ice tray on the counter.

Mrs. Edel became flustered. "It's time for *Dialing for Dollars,*" she said. She left.

When I got to Ray he was trying to close a dish towel around a pile of ice cubes. The ice was for his wrist, which was swollen so badly he couldn't close his hand. The cubes slid off the counter and over the floor. I gathered them into the towel and helped him to get the pack in place on his wrist. The right hand, the one he held the ice with, was shaking badly.

"Could you strike me a match?" he said.

He tightened his mouth to hold the cigarette straight while I lit it.

"All's well, Jumbo," he said around the cigarette.

I asked him if he wanted some breakfast. I said I would fry him an egg. Then there came a hammering at the front door. It was Mrs. Edel again.

"I am sorry to keep disturbing you and your father, but you might like to know that Governor Wallace has been shot." She leaned in to look past me. "Turn on your television."

As the three of us stood watching it in the kitchen, the phone rang— one long ring, then no more. "How strange!" Mrs. Edel said. HORSEFLY had some way of making that happen as a signal.

I took Mrs. Edel by the arm and led her out the front, across five feet of sidewalk, and up the steps to her own door. The image of Mrs. Wallace covering her fallen husband in the shopping center parking lot had frightened Mrs. Edel. "Try to settle down," I said. "The people in charge know what to do."

When I got back to the kitchen, Ray was attempting to fill a pocket flask. Bourbon was pooled across the countertop and had soaked the front of his pants. "I've made a mess of this," he said.

"You ought to lie down," I said. But he said he had to keep moving, so I carefully filled the flask for him, wiped it, and slid it into his left trouser pocket, where it clanked against his pocketknife.

"Thanks," he said. "You know what to do now, don't you?"

"Just go on as usual," I said.

He touched me on the top of my head and left out the back.

9

A *Turdus migratorius,* common name robin, made a twig nest on the light fixture outside the alley door and laid four blue eggs in it. I could see them from my window upstairs. I stuck a piece of tape across the switch so we wouldn't forget and turn the light on.

That was spring. Ray continued to be gone a lot. On May 19, the birthday of Ho Chi Minh, a bomb went off in a ladies' room at the Pentagon. I remember the date because it happens to be my birthday, too. Ray gave me a shortwave radio, a red portable set in a brown leather case. It was the best gift I have ever received, for you can hear a great variety of surprising things on the shortwaves. I scraped some ivory paint off one of the bed rails and clipped a piece of wire to the iron, and that was my auxiliary antenna. It made the static worse, but I heard my first Chinese opera. To my ears it was a lot of screaming over plinks of tin can banjos, yet it meant something to someone, and therefore I tried to follow it awhile. Then there was the woman who read out sets of numbers in Spanish for minutes on end. That meant something to someone, too.

At times the reception was better if I licked my finger and placed it on the clip. I made up a story in which my fiancé took back his proposal upon finding out that I had used my body to gather electromagnetic signals.

Ray started sleepwalking. It seemed like nothing serious. Once he let the bathtub overflow. A neighbor passed away, and some hippies got arrested for building a campfire on the sidewalk. These were some of the odds and ends of that spring on I Street.

I have said that Ray had virtually nothing to do with the fiasco at the Watergate, yet it was the reason we had to leave D.C. when we did, and in the way that we did. Here's what happened.

On the evening of June sixteenth, a Friday, Ray came home earlier than usual. He dropped a box of Chef Boyardee pizza mix on the kitchen table. "I'm taking tonight off," he said.

"Are you sick?"

"No, I'm drunk."

I set about putting the pizza together while Ray laid his head on his arms. I added a can of mushrooms to the top of the pizza to dress it up, but Ray wound up not eating any. When the pizza came out of the oven he was on the sofa, and I didn't choose to wake him. Around ten I went upstairs and got in bed with my radio on and the window open.

It was not yet daylight when someone pounded on the kitchen door from the alley. I ran down and let HORSEFLY in. He was pale and agitated. His eyes were a wreck, squinting and bleary. He stared at my hands as I measured coffee into the percolator.

Ray came into the kitchen in his socks. They spoke as though I were not there.

HORSEFLY: You and I have both got to get out of town, Ray.

RAY SLOAN: What's up?

HORSEFLY: Five of the boys from Miami have been arrested. They're in jail. The D.C. police arrested them at the Watergate.

RAY SLOAN: What happened? Did they set off an alarm?

HORSEFLY: No, there was no alarm. I don't think so. Where were you?

RAY SLOAN: Have some coffee.

HORSEFLY: My ulcers. Have you got some milk?

RAY SLOAN: Usually we do.

HORSEFLY: Some scotch?

We didn't have scotch, so HORSEFLY mixed a small shot of bourbon with his milk.

RAY SLOAN: I was ill, so I came back here.

HORSEFLY: I see. No one was watching the stairs, then.

RAY SLOAN: Where were you and GRISTLE?

HORSEFLY: We were monitoring the radio in the hotel room.

One of the men managed to signal us that they were being arrested, and then we bugged out.

RAY SLOAN: You cleaned out the room?

HORSEFLY: Pretty much.

RAY SLOAN: They can't connect you to the men they've arrested, then. The men will know to say nothing, correct?

HORSEFLY: I've got a lawyer on his way down there. There's a possibility one of the men was carrying a key to the room.

RAY SLOAN: Oops. That's a blunder. Where's my crossword?

HORSEFLY: I was hoping you had it.

RAY SLOAN: Please don't tell me you've left my crossword in the hotel room, Howard.

HORSEFLY: There's a possibility I left it in the wastebasket.

RAY SLOAN: My name is on the subscription label.

HORSEFLY: I'm glad you're feeling better now, Ray. We could have used you by the stairs. The boys had to tape the locks.

RAY SLOAN: What a screwup.

HORSEFLY: GRISTLE is very concerned that we not let this spread.

RAY SLOAN: So you make some calls from your White House phone and shut it down.

HORSEFLY: Right. I'm not too worried about it, but GRISTLE takes more of a kamikaze approach. He's raised the idea—well, I hesitate to say it in front of your girl, Ray.

I left but listened from the other side of the kitchen door.

HORSEFLY: GRISTLE has raised the idea of our all being shot on a sidewalk.

RAY SLOAN: What good would that do?

HORSEFLY: It would end the thing and contain it. He's worried the thing will get back to the campaign committee or even the President.

RAY SLOAN: Nonsense. GRISTLE wants to be shot as well?

HORSEFLY: He'll shoot himself last.

RAY SLOAN: And you believe him?

HORSEFLY: I watched him hold his arm over a candle once, just to frighten a secretary. You could smell it, Ray.

RAY SLOAN: I see. So you're leaving town.

HORSEFLY: You and I served in the big war. We've been down enough dark alleys. This would be a stupid thing to get shot over.

RAY SLOAN: Where are you intending to go?

HORSEFLY: I'm not going to tell you. It's a bugout. Just leave.

10

Ray and I left by the front door at nine in the morning. I had on my cranberry tunic dress with a ribbed white mock turtleneck under it, white socks with small dog heads on them, and my black oxford shoes. Ray wore his usual outfit, except that he'd put on a necktie under his windbreaker. We set out across New Hampshire Avenue at a stroll pace.

The sidewalks were busy with sightseers. We stopped at a bench in Lafayette Park while Ray smoked a Raleigh cigarette. The sunflower knapsack was packed to bulging on my back, causing me to perch at the front edge of the bench. I watched a man in a blue business suit kneel to pick up a quarter that had been lying heads-up on the sidewalk nearby. He glanced at me, then looked away.

"It is Christmas morning," Ray said.

In other words he felt that we were being surveilled. Ordinarily in clandestine work, when you discover you're being surveilled, you abort the operation and go home. But this was something different. I asked Ray what we were going to do.

"Let me think a minute," he said.

I felt eyes all over me, like flies on my skin. Across the street, by the White House fence, a tribe of hippie kids sat in a half circle knocking on drums. All were barefooted, with soles like tarpaper. Then the drumming stopped, and a boy in a brown corduroy suit began to read off a speech about Cambodia. He didn't think we should be bombing the North Vietnamese and Viet Cong who were headquartered there, he said. Someone in the crowd took his photograph. A few people wandered away, and the others closed in tighter.

Someone called out to the boy, "Didn't I see your face in the post office?" That won a couple of sour laughs.

Ray sat very still.

From the crowd there came a sudden shuffling of shoes. Up by the fence, one of the female hippies had brought out a gasoline can. There was a chorus of groans as she doused the head of the boy in the corduroy suit. People backed into traffic, and cars slid and stopped short. A woman ran, swinging her child by the length of his arm. It was the way you might swing a bag of laundry if for some reason you had to run away with it.

The boy in the corduroy suit sat straight and still, cross-legged and barefoot. His mop of hair was stuck flat to his skull, and the corduroy was dark where it had been soaked. The other hippies had backed their drums away to a safe distance. The girl set down the gas can and presented the boy with a book of matches.

I grabbed Ray's arm. "That boy is about to burn himself," I said. I was on my feet, but Ray held me back.

The boy produced a pipe from the pocket of his corduroy suit jacket and stuck it in his teeth MacArthur-style. He struck a match and brought the flame to the bowl, puffing at the stem as though kissing it. He worked up a good tall plume of white tobacco smoke. He snuffed out the match on a wet sleeve.

It must have been Kool-Aid in the gas can, or maybe fruit punch. The hippies were passing the can now, sipping from the spout, letting the red drink dribble down their necks.

A woman with her husband and child cried shrilly, "Is nothing serious?" To which the boy in the corduroy suit replied in a dreamy spaceman voice, "Everything's equally serious, baby."

I studied Ray's straight-nosed profile. I suppose he had guessed right away that the self-immolation scene was a bluff. Sizing up a situation fast is a skill clandestine officers live by. I saw that I would need to learn it.

Ray leaned close and said some instructions in my ear. I said them back and he nodded once, a kind of checkmark he made with his head. He stood on his cigarette.

We walked south, alongside the White House. In an upper window of the Old Executive Office Building, I saw someone in a white shirt turn his back. We cut across the Ellipse and joined the crowd on the National Mall. The atmosphere under the June a.m. sun was festival-like. A thousand human beings were on the grass, or on the straw that covered the mud, taking in the United States capital.

We had walked fully past the Natural History Museum before Ray touched my arm. We turned back and climbed the steps. Inside, several hundred small voices shouted in no particular direction. The bodies streamed in through turnstiles and eddied at the rail by the stuffed bull elephant, under the rotunda. Ray tugged me by my wrist through the churning crowd. We didn't go fast. He wanted whoever he thought was following us to keep up a little farther.

I never saw who was following us, but I am confident someone was. Ray's judgment has to be trusted on this. He taught surveillance and surveillance detection at the Farm for seven years. I believed him and still do.

In the Ice Age exhibit, a wax Cro-Magnon family stood together in furs on a hump of hard sand. The mother pressed a baby to her shoulder while the father, in a half crouch, watched into the distance. A sad, confused-looking youngster was nearby. Whoever had painted the whites of the youngster's eyes had gone outside the lines onto his eyelids, and I think that was what made him look so nutty and destitute. It was as though a sentence had begun to form inside his head. His way of life was changing, and he was unprepared.

The gallery was long and narrow. People bunched up around the signs that explained the Cro-Magnon diet and so forth. Ray grabbed me by the armpits and lifted me off the floor. He pushed me into and through the crowd. A woman gave a yelp when I kneed her. When Ray had muscled us through to the end of the gallery, he dropped me to my feet and I ducked my head.

"Arkansas," I heard him say. That was a signal meaning diverge.

I veered left like a shot down the winding staircase. The slick leather soles of my oxford shoes clicked cleanly on the dished-out marble steps.

Special hazards exist for a female in clandestine work, and one of them is the tendency of women to talk in the ladies' restroom. Back in Williamsburg, out on drills with Ray, I would sometimes go disguised as a boy or as a series of boys, and I know from experience that a nine-year-old can walk into a men's room stall with red hair and come out with his hair dark brown and no one will say a word to him or even notice, because that's how a men's room operates. A girl by herself in a ladies' room, however, is community property.

At the ladies' room on the ground floor of the Museum of Natural History, every stall was occupied and the line went out the door. I had been standing there not two seconds when a woman broke off conversation to ask me what was wrong, and four others turned to look. You see what I mean.

The point was to keep moving. I peeled the tunic dress over my head and with nine women staring got into a set of green denim overalls. I shook out a canvas shoulder bag and shoved the dress and knapsack into that, and I tucked my hair into a blue beret. I'd found the beret in a drawer of one of the ivory and gold vanities. It was ugly, but it was something I could get all my hair into. Then I left the ladies' room and slipped out the rear exit of the museum onto Constitution Avenue.

It was bright out, dazzling.

I took a cab to the Capital Hilton and passed through the cool, dim lobby. The people in chairs were inattentive, lulled by the air-conditioning. On sixteenth Avenue, where the cabs line up, I told a driver to take me to Capitol Hill. That took twelve minutes.

I walked some blocks along the row houses. The sidewalks weren't busy. If GRISTLE were to find me here, perhaps I'd be in danger, but I needed a place like this to verify that I was alone. I stopped to examine the hen-and-chick plants in someone's brick planter, then turned and walked back the way I had come, checking the few faces I passed.

I felt certain now that I had not been followed. From the corner of Second and F, I jogged to the front of Union Station. I bought a ticket, got on a train, and put my face in a copy of *Newsweek* that someone had left on the seat.

As the car filled, I counted heads. When the train moved, there were twenty-six people in it, the same as the number of letters in the alphabet.

From the knapsack I brought out a flattened wax-paper package containing a lettuce-and-baloney sandwich with mayonnaise. Somewhere in D.C. there was another one, without mayonnaise, which I hoped Ray Sloan was eating.

made the mistake of letting my thoughts wander. Where was Ray? Suppose he got held up. A person could be knocked down by a taxi while crossing the street on the way to a reconvergence, as happened to Deborah Kerr in *An Affair to Remember*. I imagined Ray hurt and myself alone in an unfamiliar city. Saliva pooled on my tongue.

I shut my eyes and breathed in a steady and deliberate fashion. I tried to think of my body as a machine that would do what I asked it to, so long as I managed it correctly. I made myself bite into my lettuce-and-baloney sandwich and chew. The vinegary smell of the mayonnaise helped me to feel better. I always bought Hellman's mayonnaise, never the store brand.

I thought the problem through. If either Ray or I did miss the reconvergence, one would signal the other by means of a simple coded message in the classified section of the *World News Digest*. Some years ago Ray had set up a prepaid account with their editorial offices in Sarasota, Florida, and I knew the phone number by heart. The *World News Digest* was available in the checkout line at any supermarket in the country. The method was reliable and secure.

I squeezed the wax paper from my sandwich into a hard ball, like a peach pit. I must have gone into a trance after that, because I jumped when the conductor touched my shoulder. "Charm City," he said.

From the platform I ran up an iron stairway to the station lobby. I found a ladies' restroom, empty this time except for two girls somewhat older than me who stood at the mirrors. One girl brushed her hair, while the other observed her dreamily. I shut myself into a stall.

The girls spoke. One had plans to buy a goldfish, and she was trying to choose a name. "Bubbles," she said. It was not a very bright idea, seeing that goldfish do not especially give off bubbles as far as I am aware. Think about that. The other girl suggested the name "Helen

Sanchez," which caused them both to gasp and scream. My, but it was awfully funny to them. They were still howling and bent, clawing at each other's sweaters, when I slipped out of the stall and pushed the green overalls into a wastebasket along with the ugly beret. I was happy to be back in my comfortable red tunic dress. The hairbrush lay on the sink rim. My own hair could have used brushing.

Like a machine built for one purpose, I walked my body across the station, dodging families and hills of luggage. I emerged into sunlight in the city of Baltimore, Maryland.

The cab at the front of the line was green. I didn't like that. The others were yellow. But you can't make them go out of order. I took the green cab downtown, then switched to a yellow one that brought me back up North Charles. I paid the driver and hopped out as he slowed for a red light. The city was new to me, but I matched up what was around me to the map in my head. I walked seven blocks in what would have looked on the map like a stairstep pattern. I passed a storefront with the words *Golden Monkey Restaurant* in cursive on the window. Next door was Lucky Bus Tour, and beyond that, an out-of-business tailor shop. I turned back. The block was empty of traffic. The time was somewhat past two in the afternoon.

Inside the Golden Monkey Restaurant I was met by a wiry, dark, mean-looking Chinese girl. She said something loud and short and had to repeat it before I understood. The phrase she kept saying was, "How many!"

I told her I was here to meet a gentleman. She led me past a carved wooden screen and some potted philodendrons to a corner where Ray sat with his back rounded and his right eye swollen almost shut.

13

"I walked into a door edge," he said. "Were you followed?"

"No."

"Good. I had my little mother with me for another half hour after we diverged. Did you see her by the elephant? She had one of those crying radio babies."

The old radio babies never cried but were little more than department-store baby dolls stuffed with batteries and electronics. There was a box full of them at the Farm. The new radio babies will cry and writhe.

"She handed me off when I came back onto the Mall. Then she picked me up again at the National Gallery."

"How did you finally lose her?"

"I had some cabs waiting. It was pretty easy. These people have the resources of professionals, but they don't stick on you like professionals."

There had been dozens of babies in that museum, but the only one I'd paid attention to was the Cro-Magnon baby made of wax. I was about to ask Ray who "these people" were when, from around the carved wooden screen, the mean-looking Chinese girl shot out and set a glass of beer in front of him. She gave me a hard, silent appraisal, turning away just as I was asking for a Pepsi. I felt the insult to be deliberate.

She fit in pretty well with the seedy ambience of the Golden Monkey. The floor was gritty, and the heart-leaf philodendrons were dying of thirst in their pots. It takes some serious negligence to kill that plant. Anyway, we were there. Ray was sweating a lot. He dabbed at his forehead with a red cloth napkin, using care around the swollen eye.

"Here is the point," he said when I finally got my question out.

"Anyone we know, we must avoid. Friends and former colleagues, neighbors, everybody. But especially GRISTLE. Can we let it go at that?"

"I know GRISTLE wants to kill us," I confessed.

"What are you talking about?"

"I heard it through the door. He wants us shot on the sidewalk so we can't tell about the Watergate."

Ray shook his head. "Jumbo," he said.

"You didn't tell me not to listen."

"First of all, nobody wants to shoot *you*. He might want to shoot *me*, but—"

"That's worse!" I started to break up at this point, against my will.

"It's not going to happen," Ray said. "It won't happen. We're safe, okay? This joker was trained by the FBI, for heaven's sake."

"You're not afraid of the FBI?"

"Oh, no. Not in the least. Go to any post office and look at the slobs they have on the most-wanted list. If they can't catch a bunch of hippies who bombed the Pentagon, how are they going to catch us?"

"I don't know."

"Well, they're not. Tell me you're not scared."

"I'm not scared."

"Good. And if you do see GRISTLE, run the other way."

A Chinese man in sleek black slacks and a V-neck pullover came to speak to Ray. His bald, shiny sternum showed in the V. Ray addressed him as Mr. Wang. He had cauliflower cheeks.

We rose and followed Mr. Wang through the kitchen and out the back. Down the alley a steel door was propped open by means of a rubber mat folded on top of itself. Mr. Wang waved us in, kicking the mat and closing the door. We were inside Lucky Bus Tour.

We passed a mop and a coat rack. Wang rapped on a door, and the answer came as a kind of bark. Again Wang motioned us in, only this time he didn't follow.

14

There was a camera on a tripod and a small steel desk with another Chinese male behind it. A tassel beard of forty black hairs grew off his chin. He came close in order to scrutinize Ray's face. He held a desk lamp on one side of Ray's head, then the other, studying the swollen eye.

"Her, too?"

"Yes," Ray said.

"How old is she? Twelve?"

"She's eighteen."

"She might be fifteen. No more than that, I think."

His English was better than Wang's. He gave me the lamp treatment, then nodded at my knapsack. "Have you got some makeup in there, miss?"

"No."

He opened a desk drawer and brought out a greasy tackle box, which he laid in my hands. He sent me to a small, grim lavatory.

There was my face in the cloudy mirror. Fatigue makes an adult look older, but it makes a child look younger and more childish. The skin under my eyes had a gray shine to it, and the knit forehead didn't help.

I put a lot of beige powder all over my face and ears, used a pencil around my eyes, and smeared some lipstick onto my mouth. I tried a few things with my hair, but it is the kind of hair that lies fairly slick no matter what is done to it. There was a comb in the tackle box, but I was unwilling to handle it. I pulled some hair forward to cover the sides of my face.

When Ray saw me he said, "Oh, that's not good." I thought I had better go wash my face off, but the Chinese man said we'd try a picture first. He put me on a stool in front of some blue paper taped to the wall and snapped a Polaroid. Then he took another with the hair pulled even farther forward so that all but a three-inch strip down the middle of my face was covered with my hair. In the picture, I did not look older so much as embalmed. Well, but that was a strategy. The thing in the picture was ageless.

On the desk he spread out a dozen driver's licenses from various states. The idea was to choose the ones that would need to be altered the least.

The faces had a sad foolishness about them. I suppose it is hard not to look foolish in your driver's license picture once it has been stolen from you. All of the licenses were current. They included a set of three that belonged to a husband, wife, and daughter, judging by their names and by the way the young woman resembled both of the older people, who did not, however, resemble each other, except that all three of them were black.

Ray had his mind made up on licenses from a southern state. "Don't you have a couple from Tennessee?" he said.

"No. I could get a couple."

"Okay, get a couple."

The man said it would take him one week.

Wang had waited in the alley. As he led us back through the kitchen, the mean-looking girl was receiving a good, loud scolding in Chinese from a gray-haired woman with an iron pot in her hand. The girl faced a few degrees to one side, as though to let the high-pitched coughing fit of language be deflected.

"My mother took the girl on for charity," Wang said. "She is dull. Speaks no English, very little Chinese."

"What does she speak?" Ray asked.

"A little Cantonese, that is all. We have a lot of trouble with that simpleminded girl."

I twisted to get one more look at her and saw an interesting thing. The hard eyes that had at first seemed calculating and full of foreign malice now struck me as merely stolid and flat. There was something to learn in this. I had seen a face I couldn't read and attributed cunning to it. It never occurred to me that her face might be unreadable because she had been dropped on her head as a baby.

Wang left us at our table. When the girl came out again, a little pinker for being shouted at, Ray ordered more beer and a large meal of Chinese food, taking care to include the number of each menu item and see that the girl wrote it down. It was a relief to know she was simpleminded. That made it easier to put up with her slow pace and sullen manner. Ray left her an oversized tip, as was his habit whatever the service.

15

Outside in the sun Ray patted himself for a matchbook. A cab-driver welcomed us to "Baldimore" and drove us out Harford Road to a used car dealer.

Ray liked a sky-blue Plymouth Scamp with a white vinyl top, but the salesman balked when Ray mentioned a test drive. "Maybe you've been drinking," the salesman said.

"I didn't mean that *I* would drive the car," Ray said. "My daughter will drive it."

"I can't allow that," the salesman said.

"Why? She's perfectly sober."

"What is she, twelve?"

"Why don't we let the salesman drive?" I suggested.

"I'm busy," the salesman said.

Ray brought a thick stack of hundred-dollar bills from his wind-breaker pocket. The paper was so crisp and springy, it would hardly stay folded.

This caused the salesman to change his tune. Ray got in front on the passenger side, and I got in back by myself.

"I'm Armando Snacki," the salesman said.

"Show us what the car is capable of, Mr. Snacki," Ray said.

Armando Snacki accelerated evenly and took us through a few smooth turns. Ray closed his eyes and fell asleep. We were pulling a slow U-turn when the tires squealed and Ray woke up. He twisted and looked at me.

"We are test-driving a Plymouth Scamp," I reminded him.

He touched his mouth, checking for a cigarette.

Back at the lot, Ray told Armando Snacki that we would take the Plymouth, but only with a new set of tires thrown in. "Those you have on there are noisy."

Snacki capitulated. "I can't sell it to anyone else, now that it smells like egg rolls."

I had carried a paper sack of egg rolls from the Golden Monkey. He was right, there was a smell.

I drank a 7-Up while the tires got put on. Ray gave Snacki some hundreds. Then the car was brought around front, and Ray got in on the passenger side again.

I reminded him I'd never driven a car.

"It isn't hard," he said. "I will explain it right now."

16

"All I need to give you are a few simple principles," Ray said. "Number one concerns your feet. The right foot is for going and stopping. Does this car have a clutch?"

We established that it didn't.

"In this car, let your left foot rest. On rare occasions, you will use your left knee to hold the steering wheel, for example if you are eating food.

"Principle two: avoid left turns, and avoid reverse. Principle three: adjust your mirrors."

Ray got out and stood in several positions around the car while I moved the mirrors so I could see him. Armando Snacki stood at the plate glass of his office.

Ray got back in the car. "Don't ever let the fuel level drop below half a tank. Top it off at the end of the day. Every week, check the oil. To check the brake lights by yourself, back up to a wall. Carry spare bulbs in the glove compartment, and carry a screwdriver. *Don't* give some bored police officer a reason to pull you over. The first thing he'll want is your license, and then there goes our cover. Above all, we must not go to Tennessee. It would be the worst place in the world for us, once we get our fake Tennessee driver's licenses."

"We have no reason to ever go to Tennessee."

"Correct. Let's drive."

I got the Scamp started and put it in gear. When I lifted my foot from the brake, the car moved, and I stomped the brake again.

Armando Snacki came out of his building.

"Keep moving," Ray said. "We're done with Armando Snacki."

I raised my foot off the brake, and we idled through a wide turn across the lot. I did have to use the reverse gear once, when I came to a light pole. I aimed us out the exit. Then we were off. I was driving a car.

I had to corkscrew down on the seat in order to reach the pedals. I used my left leg to keep from sliding into the floor.

Ray flagged a liquor store. "Stop there, if you would."

It was on our left, across three lanes of traffic. Remembering principle two, I got us into the liquor store parking lot by a series of seven right turns.

"Leave it running," Ray said.

My hands and armpits were sweating. Wouldn't some country lane be a better place for my first driving lesson? But I decided to trust Ray on it, and when he came back, I drove again. He set two fifths in the floor and opened a pint to hold in his lap. "You are doing just fine with your driving," he said.

We took a two-room apartment at the Fletcher Hotel on St. Paul and Madison. The front room contained one olive-colored sofa, one folding chair, and a card table with a hot plate on it. The black grime on the hot plate was hard like a casing. There was a bedroom and a minuscule bathroom. On the floor beside the toilet, someone had left behind a Donald Duck orange juice lid.

Ray settled in on the sofa with his two bottles of bourbon and three packs of Raleighs. The pint was gone. "I need a favor," he said.

"What is it?"

He held out one of the bottles. "Hide this somewhere."

"This place is kind of small for hiding things," I said.

He closed his eyes.

I hid the bottle in my knapsack. Then I rinsed out the sink and brushed my teeth with a lot of toothpaste. I got in the bed.

I had brought the shortwave radio, and I managed to pull in a few minutes of the Voice of America. Americans are not meant to hear it, since the government is not supposed to propagandize its own citizens, but sometimes you can hear it anyway, depending on the sunspots. The program I heard was a course in English. A woman and man were demonstrating how to have a conversation about the contents of the newspaper. For example,

MAN: Did you see today's headlines?
WOMAN: Yes, I saw today's headlines.
MAN: Tomorrow is Election Day. Have you chosen your can-
  didate?
WOMAN: I will vote for the candidate from the Blue Party.
MAN: Beef is on sale at the Robinson Market.
WOMAN: The Robinson Market has good beef.

It was a modest sort of propaganda. Pro-voting, pro-beef. The voices were furred over with soft static. Sometimes a long whistle echoed up from the bottom of a well.

Later I woke to footsteps. The bedroom door was open, though I thought I remembered closing it.

An egg of light moved low against the baseboard and onto the pocked gray linoleum. It shot up to the ceiling and stopped there, jumping in place just slightly.

"Ray?"

He stepped in. I couldn't see him well behind the flashlight he carried, but I knew his sigh.

He moved the light down the wall to the foot of the bed. The batteries were getting low. He ran the light over the bedspread until it glowed in my face.

"The bottle is in my knapsack," I said.

He didn't respond to that. With a flick he made the egg of light snap across the ceiling.

"Like that," he said.

"What are you talking about?"

"That is how they moved," he said.

He did it again, snapping it from one end of the ceiling to the other. The egg halted weightlessly against one wall then the other. Ray seemed to study it in a purposeful way.

Then he turned the light onto himself. He was holding the blade of his sodbuster pocketknife alongside his throat. "Don't let me do it," he said.

I jumped out of bed and grabbed his arm. I managed to pry a couple fingers open and shook the knife to the floor. "Wake up," I said.

He shook his head at me.

"You're asleep!" I said. "Wake up!" I steered him to the sofa and sat him down. "You were walking in your sleep, Ray!"

I sat with him and he closed his eyes. He was quiet. Then he got up and ran into the bathroom. An awful croaking noise came out. He was throwing up.

"You need to drink some water," I said through the door.

"Go to bed," he slurred back at me.

We didn't have even a paper cup to put some water in. I told him to cup his hands at the faucet and drink some water.

I heard splashing, so maybe he did what I said.

He came out and lay back on the sofa. "Dear God," he said. "I'm falling apart."

There was honking on St. Paul, and a gray metallic light came in at the window. The street was lit all night, and the blind was broken and wouldn't stay closed.

"You shouldn't have to be a part of this," Ray said.

"It's all right. We're in close quarters for a while."

"It's not all right. I have let you down badly, Jumbo."

"You haven't let me down *in the least*," I said.

I touched his forehead. It was hot and dry. There were about a hundred things I wanted to tell him—mostly things I had guessed that I wasn't supposed to have guessed, or things I remembered that I don't think he knew I remembered. I wanted him to know that I was sturdy, and that he needn't protect me from the truth.

"Rely on me," I said.

He made an odd noise. A squeak. I couldn't see his face well, and half a minute went by before I understood that he was crying. It startled me, because I'd never seen him cry before. I went all to pieces, then, and had to go to the other room. I was crying so hard I was wheezing. My bare foot hit Ray's pocketknife. I closed it up and pushed it under the mattress. The flashlight was dead. I pinched myself on the legs.

I ran back to Ray. "We're all right!" I said. "Let's get things in order. We need some paper cups! We'll cover that window. Also, you need some pajamas. You're sleeping in your clothes! No wonder you're up at night. Did you drink from your hands like I told you to?" I went on fussing over him in this way while sniffling. "I'm going out right now to find some paper cups," I said.

"You won't find them this time of night."

"Where's that empty bottle? You can drink from that."

"I'll be sick again," he said.

I rinsed out his handkerchief and folded it over his forehead. "I know you'll feel better in the morning," I said.

"Maybe. You should go back to bed."

But I stayed. I sat on the edge of the sofa while he lay there taking shallow, quick breaths. I held his hand, which was not a thing I often did. I can't think when I had done it before. His hand was big. I held it in both of mine.

18

Eventually he slept. Where does a person go, when he's asleep? It's a pointless question, but I felt he had left me and gone somewhere else. Yet I wasn't quite alone, because there was traffic noise from outside, and the occasional raised voice or door slam reached my ears from somewhere else in the Fletcher Hotel. I stepped around the room just taking things in. It was night and the lights were off. The off-white walls were off-blue in patches of glare from the street. The room was weirdly large and barren with Ray on his back on the low green sofa, and the flimsy card table adrift in the middle of the floor.

I went to the bedroom and lay down.

When I woke up again it was daylight and Ray was still asleep. I was hungry, so I went out by myself to find food. I made a childish blunder at a place called Carrelli's Market on St. Paul. I had a dollar and change in the pocket of my knapsack and had calculated the amount to be sufficient for two coffees and two large cinnamon rolls sealed in crisp plastic. When I got to the counter the girl gave me a total that was somewhat over that. I had left out the sales tax, and I had to put back one of the cinnamon rolls. It's the sort of thing that takes you down a grade or two in your own mind. It bothered me even though they were great big cinnamon rolls. Too big, really. We could split the one.

The emotional scene from the night before had knocked me off my balance. Ray and I really were not given to that kind of eruption. I put it behind me. On the street, white sunlight filtered through a pillowy haze. Sand had washed over the sidewalk from a construction site. Trucks were making deliveries, drowning out the birds.

When I let myself into the room, Ray was sitting up.

"Where have you been?" he said.

"I brought breakfast," I said.

"What's your name?" He meant my cover name—the new one.

"Roberta Dewey."

"Who's the old guy you're staying with?"

"Roy McJones."

"'Roy McJones.' Why are you with that old guy?"

"I'm his private nurse."

"You attended nursing school where?"

"I'm not a *registered* nurse. I look after Mr. McJones."

"What's wrong with him that he needs a private nonregistered nurse looking after him day and night? Can't he wipe his own nose?"

"Would you like your nurse to go around describing your medical conditions?"

"I see. All right. Anyway, you look awfully young to be someone's nurse. You say you're nineteen?"

"Maybe it *is* a stretch to say I'm nineteen, Ray."

"Not at all." He touched his hurt eye carefully. The swelling was mostly gone. "You do need to have some patter ready, though."

"My growth was stunted by a disease in childhood," I improvised.

"What disease in childhood?"

"Compound complex anemia."

"We'll work on it."

He rubbed his fingers together now, looking for a cigarette. They were in his jacket pocket, but we couldn't find the jacket. It was a big mystery, since the room was a nearly empty box.

"Listen up," he said. "We need a case officer, bad."

"Okay."

"It'll have to be you."

"I don't know how to be a case officer, Ray."

"Well, of course you don't. Nobody knows how to be a case officer until he has been instructed in how to do it. Which was my job for some time, you'll recall."

"Oh."

He laughed. "You have an excellent deadpan."

"Thanks, I guess."

"Did you know they gave me a medal when I retired?"

"No, I didn't know."

"We had a little ceremony where they showed it to me. Then they put it in a safe."

"I wish I'd been there."

"You didn't miss much. Hey, Jumbo, where are my cigarettes?"

I went looking in the bedroom, because that was the only other place I could think to look. I looked under the bed. Why? There was a sock under there, which I didn't touch. It had an evil, hardened look about it. When I came up I felt compelled to wash my hands and face, and I did so.

When I got back to Ray I found him smoking. "The jacket was on the floor behind the sofa," he said. "Thanks for breakfast." The sugar-smeared plastic sleeve that had held the one giant cinnamon roll was on the cushion beside him, empty.

"All of what I'm about to tell you is secret," Ray began.

I listened.

"The case officer is the person who handles the spies, and there is a method to it. First, he has an intelligence requirement. He doesn't just go out sniffing the air. He starts with some specific question. How many working fire trucks in Hanoi? The answer is a piece of information. That is number one.

"Number two, he wants to *identify a person* who can get this information. Let me repeat that. *Identify a person* who has access to the information that will answer the intelligence requirement. Who could it be?"

"The fire chief?"

"Maybe so. Number three. The case officer is going to *study that person*. Study him. Here, you don't know what will be important. Tell me your name again."

"Roberta."

"Good. This step of *studying the person* is often the step that will separate an effective case officer from an ineffective one. Some questions you might ask yourself regarding the prospective asset include, what is this person's day like? What is a good day for him? What would be a terrific day? What would make his day very bad?

"Does he wait with his kid for the bus in the morning? Do they talk, or do they just stand there? Does he turn away as the bus is leaving, or does he stay and watch it go? Watching it go is a sign of fear. Well, what's he afraid of? Of course, you want to form some rough ideas about his money situation. You won't necessarily need to see his bank account. A look at his shoes might be enough.

"What you are seeking is a need or urgent desire that you are able to satisfy. Sometimes you will find it ready-made. For instance, a relative needs medical care. There are bills. You can help. Or you may induce the person to feel a need that he has not felt before. Here's one. His oldest child seems bright enough—wouldn't he like to send that child to private school? Ship her off someplace safe and plush like Switzerland?

"When you have identified your person's vulnerability is when you begin to *develop* him as an asset. You've met—now become friends. Ask him to do you a medium-sized favor. It ought to be something that causes him a certain inconvenience. And if he has to bend a rule to do it, so much the better. In return you will buy him lunch. Knowing the lunch is owed to him will help him enjoy it. You are developing an *involvement*, you see.

"Soon he'll have begun to figure some things out. But by the time he guesses what's happening, he'll find that he's already involved and has been for a good while. Seeing you means something to him. You never part without having arranged your next meeting. Because he is *involved*, he wants you to succeed and be happy. And here is something very important: *you want him to be happy as well.*

"Finally, you make the pitch. That's all there is to it, really. Your first intelligence requirement is this: I want the names of all our neighbors in this wretched hotel."

He went into the bathroom and shut the door.

20

In the daytime the lobby of the Fletcher Hotel was seldom empty. Idle men filled it. One had the sense that these were men each of whom was between two things. It showed in a new set of freshly pressed secondhand clothes, or else in the way a man shaved and carefully wet-combed his hair, only to stand in one place all morning looking at the rug. Had his life come apart, and was he afraid to sit alone upstairs? Or maybe it was the reverse: his life had hardened into something he didn't like anymore, and he was waiting for an idea of how to break it.

I passed through the lobby at intervals of ninety minutes. I would wander down St. Paul for fruit, gum, or cigarettes, then come back through. The men watched me with a steady, low-grade attention. Around dark, things jumped. The quiet men, the time-passers, were replaced by those who wanted to talk and be seen. A giant in a leather vest and white cowboy hat held court inside the vestibule. In place of charisma he had a loud voice and the hat. The desk shift changed at eleven. I went to bed, setting the alarm for three.

At five after three I was back downstairs. The lobby was empty except for the night clerk behind his grate, a heavyset male with big brown widely spaced eyes and a pink mouth. He wore a black turtleneck. His hair was thin on top, though he couldn't have been past thirty. I introduced myself as Roberta Dewey from Room 33.

He asked whether there was a problem with the room.

"It's no palace."

He stared at me, then went back to running his dull pencil over a page of notebook paper.

"Do you work here every night?" I asked.

"Every night."

"What is your day like?"

He twitched on his tall stool. "I get up at eight to follow my jogging program. Then I mop the floor, and then I pray and levitate, and then I eat some whole grains and fruits. Then I come here."

I studied him. The black turtleneck couldn't hide his soft cheeks and round chin. His color was poor, too. He was no fitness enthusiast. He had the face of a sad boy-king in a dungeon. The wide-set brown eyes gave him an amphibian aspect.

"You don't like your job," I said.

He laughed. "Who would?"

"It seems easy enough. You register people and check them out. Call a cab now and then."

"Why are you here?"

I gave him my cover story.

"You're his *nurse*?"

"That's right."

"I'd say he likes watching you cross the room."

"Would you like to come out here and repeat that?"

"Don't get touchy!" he said.

"Look. I'm fond of Mr. McJones, but it isn't the way you think. He's like an uncle to me."

"Whatever you say."

His voice had gone soft. I'd made a mistake in getting angry.

"Tell me something," I said. "What would be a terrific day for you?"

"A day when nobody yells at me would be nice."

"Does the pay from this job meet your needs?"

"I've adjusted my needs to fit the pay. The job gives me time to compose."

"Compose what?"

His nostrils flared with contempt, but his eyes clung to mine. He spun the notebook and slid it through an opening in the grate. It was a cheap, school-style notebook. The wide-ruled pages held poem after poem in broad, dull pencil strokes. He pulled the notebook back. "They're not for kids to read," he said.

"Who does read them?"

He turned away from me, straightening stacks of paper behind his grate. His cheeks had big blotches on them now. He was blushing.

I had identified his vulnerability.

21

Poetry was never my thing, but on Monday morning at the Enoch Pratt Free Library I got myself a quick education. I even memorized a poem. It wasn't hard.

The night clerk's newtlike eyes blinked at me when I let him know my intention of reciting a poem. "It will be a sonnet by Sir Thomas Wyatt." I said it through.

He wore a small, wry smile on his mouth. He raised his black eyebrows and let his head loll about like a heavy flower. "A medieval war poem," he said.

"Not at all." I showed him how the poem described a lover attempting to hide his passionate feelings. The "flag" is the color that appears in his face, betraying his "position." It was not a difficult business to work out. "Anyway, what is your name?" I said.

"Henry" was all he gave me. I didn't push for more. He was busy not seeming impressed. And yet he asked me to say the poem again. I did it.

He frowned and appeared agitated. I let him think.

He began scribbling. Soon he said, "Here's one by William Shakespeare. I've written it out so I won't mix the words up."

He read it to me. Toward the end of this short poem Henry began to *whisper*. Something in the poem moved him. But he read the final two lines out loud in an offhand way, as though to break the poem's dangerous spell.

I said, "What about an extra set of sheets, Henry? I've got Roy McJones in bed all day up there."

"But of course, my little friend," he said, and he slid down from his stool. It was a long way down for him. There was something wrong with his legs.

When he got back, he pushed a frayed but clean set of sheets across the counter.

"Thanks, Henry. I'm aware that caused you a certain inconvenience, not to mention that you probably had to bend a rule."

"It's no inconvenience. And you're allowed to have all the sheets you want."

"Mm. I seem to have left my key upstairs."

"I can lend you one."

He opened a shallow steel cabinet and took a key from hook number thirty-three. There was one more key on that hook. I asked him to give me that one, too.

"Sorry, I can't. That *is* a rule."

"I want to tell you something in confidence, Henry. Roy McJones has got acute paranoia. That's why we couldn't stay in Bethesda anymore. He thought Mrs. McJones was putting antifreeze in his grenadine! If he should find out there is one extra key to Room 33 down here lying on a hook waiting to get borrowed so someone can slip into his room and poison or molest him, he will have us pack and go no matter what time of day or night it is."

Henry blinked softly at me. "But *you're* not paranoid, are you?"

"I see your point. I don't *have* to tell McJones about the key. But I promised him that I would never, ever lie about duplicate keys. I like to honor promises."

With a shrug Henry handed it over. "Boss will have my skin when he sees that hook empty," he said.

"Put any spare key on there. Your boss won't check the number."

He did as I suggested. There was my medium-sized favor.

In return I let him read me some original verse from his notebook. Just as Ray had predicted, earning his favor had put Henry into a happy mood. He chattered brightly as he picked the yellow foil wrapper from a cube of chicken bouillon. He stood the cube on a page of his notebook and it waited there, naked, while the water in the electric kettle got hot.

"You have a decent ear for poetry," Henry said. "You'll like this next one."

But it was time for the pitch. "Look here, Henry. I need a list of all persons registered on the third floor. McJones can't sleep without it. Will you help me?"

He blinked the big, moist eyes with their speckled irises. He showed me the guest register. There were fewer than two dozen names for the whole five-story hotel. I copied them down.

"Okay, Henry. Read me the one I'm going to like."

Later that night, Ray and I considered whether we ought to seal the relationship with a small cash payment. It would deepen Henry's involvement with us, but suppose the extra money led him to quit his job as night clerk.

"There is often a temptation to give more than you have to," Ray said. "A good case officer gets inside his agent's world, finds the thing that is missing, and gives only that."

We agreed we had a better prospect in Henry if I simply kept listening to his poems.

Ray looked over the list of names again. "It is your first recruitment and a good one," he said.

22

Because of his cover as a paranoid schizophrenic shut-in, Ray wasn't going out at all. I did the errands, such as buying paper dishware and a blue enamel dripolator at the Marquis Variety Store on Howard Street. I moved the Scamp once a day to keep it from getting ticketed. The idea was to lie low and let the week pass, then get our new IDs and drive west, maybe to Colorado.

Ray didn't seem to mind his confinement much. He took to it as though it were a natural phase. He worked the crossword puzzle in the *World News Digest* when the new one came out, and he read and reread each story relating to the arrests at the Watergate building. We saw HORSEFLY's name on the front of *The New York Times*. His White House phone number—the same one he'd jotted on a corner of my place mat—had turned up in an address book carried by one of the burglars. The *Times* described him as the mastermind of the Bay of Pigs invasion.

"The hell he was," Ray said.

I asked him what was the purpose of the break-in.

"That's like asking what is the purpose of seven thousand nuclear warheads in Europe."

"What *is* the purpose of seven thousand nuclear warheads in Europe?"

"If a thing can happen, it'll happen," he said. "In fact, it probably has."

"I still don't understand."

"I don't, either," Ray said. "This idea of electronic surveillance has really grabbed ahold of someone's imagination. In the old days it was all about human assets. It's true, the bugs are cleaner, because you don't have that chain of personalities all groping each other. Bear in mind, this is an old man with a very bad headache talking."

"I'll get some aspirin," I said.

"The problem is, we keep changing presidents. Each one has to prove himself. And it's a shame, because democracy—well, you'd prefer to be in favor of it. But nowadays we change presidents so often, the fellows never get the chance to settle in. They get in there, you know, and naturally the first thing they have to do is try all the buttons out. 'What does *this* button do?' 'Well, push it and find out, sir.' Hell, I'd do the same if it were me. And then something happens, some real or imagined insult, and the President considers that sand has been kicked in his face. *Hey, skinny, your ribs are showing.* Therefore, you better believe some buttons are going to get pushed. Now, you take your average dictator or king. They do get mean as hell after fifteen or twenty years, but they settle, okay? They get to where they don't have to prove anything, because they just don't care anymore, which is in a way healthy. There is a pragmatism that comes with that. We haven't had a president really settle down since Franklin Roosevelt."

"But what was the intelligence requirement? What was HORSEFLY looking for?"

"That I don't know. National security—it's never good to ask a lot of questions. The cynics are calling it campaign hijinks, of course."

"I don't understand."

"Well, viewing it from an un-nuanced outside perspective, they think Nixon was seeking some sort of election advantage."

I considered what he was saying. "Wouldn't that be illegal?"

"I think it would be, Jumbo."

I made out a shopping list. Aspirin, something for lunch. Ray's two bottles of bourbon were long gone. I mentioned that.

"I'll try drying out awhile," he said.

"Is that a good idea right now?"

"Why not?"

I could tell he was surprised that I questioned him on it. Half an odd smile slanted across his mouth. He was on edge, though, and chattier than usual, and somehow loose. He'd turned the linings of his pockets out. How long did he mean to leave them that way?

I took a long walk to Lexington Market, where fish, hats, vegetables, knives, and candy were sold from the stalls. I bought some good-sized fried chicken thighs for forty cents apiece. Breasts were selling for fifty-five. It was fine with me because I prefer the thigh.

When I got back to the Fletcher it was after one-thirty. I found Ray sitting on the sofa barefooted, tapping or rather slapping both feet on the wooden floor. There was an awful scorched smell in the room. He'd left the hot plate on under the dripolator and burned the pot dry.

"I smoked up all my cigarettes, too," he said.

I had left a new pack in his windbreaker pocket, but I saw from the overflowing ashtray that he had already found that one. I got a pack from the machine in the lobby, then arranged the chicken thighs and some mashed sweet potatoes on our paper plates. Ray smoked a cigarette, and we ate our late lunch.

"Thank you for this meal," he said. He looked away when I looked at him. Something was wrong, but I couldn't tell what.

"I shouldn't have you eating lunch so late," I said.

"I'm dizzy," he said.

I was on my feet to bring him a cup of water when a knock came at the door.

23

It was Henry.

"What do you want?" I said. He'd surprised me, and my tone was off.

"Are you coming to see me tonight?"

"Of course, Henry. After I get Mr. McJones settled."

I stood holding the door. Henry wanted more from me. I could see him trying to bend his newtlike gaze past my arm to look inside.

From behind me Ray said, "I don't feel so good." I twisted to see him standing over me, his chin shiny with chicken grease. "Who are you?" he said to Henry.

"I'm the one who's showing her the guest register."

Ray groaned.

I stepped out into the hall and shut the door. "I should have explained something, Henry. It is important that we not be seen together except at the front desk. Someone could get the wrong idea about our relationship, or rather the right idea, if you follow me."

"I have a new poem to read you tonight."

"I'll be there. I look forward to hearing this poem."

"All right. McJones looks kind of crazy."

"Because he is."

Henry gave me a long, wondering look before moving away carefully down the dirty stairs. He held tightly to the banister.

I went in all ready to congratulate Ray on his crazy act but found him stretched out on the sofa, hugging his stomach. "Something bad, bad, bad was in that chicken," he said.

I rinsed out a handkerchief to wipe his face. Within an hour things were much worse. He paced, hunched almost double, then stretched out on his back twisting, and then began to mutter about birds and turtles. I gave him some aspirin. He chewed the tablets, then spit them on the floor and lunged into the bathroom.

He began to shiver awfully. His jaw clamped, and the muscles churned on the sides of his face. He pulled his pants and shirt off and wrapped himself in sheets. Soon the sheets were soaked with sweat.

I felt okay. The chicken hadn't affected my stomach in any bad way.

Of course. It wasn't the chicken at all.

24

In the liquor store across St. Paul, the old man with a bandage on his ear refused to sell to me.

"It's for my boss," I explained.

He shook his head.

Down the sidewalk, I spotted Henry at the dollar table outside a secondhand book shop. He wasn't reading the books but smelling them, one after another.

"I need a favor," I said.

He blinked at me, gathering his wits. He hadn't seen me coming, and his wits were widely scattered. "You said we're not supposed to meet away from the desk."

"This is urgent!" I gave him some cash and instructions. "I would do it myself, but I've misplaced my driver's license."

Henry scuttled off down the sidewalk. He didn't buy my story, but he didn't need to anymore. He was docile and compliant now. I had him "under discipline," as it is called in the trade. He was back to me in no time with a pint of something called Old Overholt. I left him with his fragrant dollar books.

At the room I had some trouble locating Ray. I heard snapping and at last found him in a space between the bed and the wall. He was down there wrapped in his wet sheets, snapping his fingers first by one ear, then the other.

He wanted me to look inside both his ears with the flashlight. He thought there was a "bug" stuck in one of them. I don't know what kind of bug he meant, the electronic kind or the kind with six legs. I dreaded whatever I might see, but I looked, because he wanted me to. I could not see far in for all of the iron-colored hair that was growing in his ears.

I poured some bourbon into a paper coffee cup with a little water. I told him to drink it.

He sipped it, and you'd have thought I had given him poison. He threw the cup against the wall.

"What are you trying to do to me?" he said.

"This has happened to you before," I said. "It happened at the Farm. I know about it."

"Somebody left that chicken sitting out!" He said it in language that was spotted with profanities. I've omitted those.

"Ray," I said. "Settle down, okay? *Settle.*" I moved closer to him. He was still wedged down there in between the bed and the wall, all of him from the chest down.

He covered his face with the sheet.

"I know what's happening, Ray." I tried to make my voice very flat, because a girl can sound simpering or overly plaintive when she is emotional. "It happened at the Farm when you stopped drinking. They kept you in the infirmary for two weeks. Do you remember?"

He didn't move.

"I know I'm not supposed to know about it. It happened over Christmas break, when the school was closed. I stayed with the Gandys that week, and Mrs. Gandy explained it to me. If a person is used to having several drinks every day, sometimes he'll need a doctor's care if he suddenly stops. You can get very sick from just stopping."

Still Ray didn't respond or move.

"I want you to know that I didn't mind spending that week with the Gandys," I said. "Christmas is a stupid holiday. I only mention it because I'm concerned that this project of giving up drinking is not a good project for us to be taking on right now. We need to save that for a time when you have access to plenty of fresh air and vitamins. You are missing your long daily walks, too. Your whole routine has been wrecked. Let's do this right. I sent Henry to buy this bourbon, Ray. He'll do anything I tell him to now. I've got him well under control. It's not your regular brand, but I'm sure it'll do. Are you hearing me, Ray? Please, uncover your head."

He brought the sheet down from his face. His face was pale as milk, and his eyes were messy and wet. I recovered the paper cup he had thrown and dusted off the rim. I poured a couple swallows of bourbon in and diluted it with water from the sink. I gave him the cup and he drank it down obediently.

We both waited in place to see what would happen. No evil ghosts came writhing out. He blinked a few times, and then he sighed and raised his eyebrows. He started to cough, and I lit him a Raleigh, which he climbed out from behind the bed and sat up to smoke. Then he had a few more swallows of the Old Overholt, and then he drank some water, ate a Captain's Wafer, and was quiet. I felt like we were out of the woods for a while.

25

Late that night, when I had Ray laid out on the couch and sleeping, I went downstairs to let Henry read me his new poem. It concerned a bodiless male personage who was in love with a fetching librarian, only he couldn't kiss, caress, or even say good morning to her because he was a bodiless personage. All he could do was hover in the stacks, a dusty spirit, and get a load of her shelving books all day long.

"It's poignant," I said.

Henry gave me a long, big-eyed look. He was on his high stool inside his cage, and I stood at the opening in the grate. It was two in the morning.

"Did Mr. McJones enjoy his cocktail?"

"Why do you ask?"

"You said it was urgent." He blinked at me slowly.

Out on St. Paul there were tire squeals and shouting. A man ran into the lobby, looked around him, and ran back out.

Then quiet.

"I had better go back up and check on Roy McJones," I said.

"All right." Henry pushed the guest register through and I copied the few new names into my notebook.

"See you tomorrow night," I said.

"Good night, Roberta," he said sadly.

I started toward the stairs. But I wasn't really done for the night and I knew it, because I recalled Ray's admonition on managing an asset: *you want him to be happy as well.* I went back to the cage.

"What's got you down, Henry?"

"I can't really talk about it," Henry said.

"Isn't there something I can do to help?"

"Yes."

"What, then?"

"I can't tell you!"

"I'm no good with puzzles," I said.

He asked me whether the librarian in his poem reminded me of anyone. "Dark eyebrows and yellow hair? 'Small and cruelly efficacious hands'?"

"She sounds like a pill. I don't know why the bodiless personage is in love with her like that."

His eyes looked past me into several thousand miles of space. "I was wrong, you have no ear for poetry," he said.

Well, I had tried. I went on upstairs.

26

Things were different with Ray now. He stayed in bed for four days, eating nothing but crackers and tangerines that I peeled for him. He slept a lot. Sometimes we talked.

"You're a good kid," he said.

I wouldn't have minded hearing that sort of thing, except that there was something sad in the way he said it.

"You've seen my less attractive side," he added.

His tone was confidential and beaten. I couldn't seem to convince him that we might wind up better off for having left D.C. "I've never told you this, but I don't have a very high opinion of the D.C. public schools," I said.

"Is that right?"

"I think we can do much better. We've got to keep it together here until we have our new identities, and then we'll start fresh out West."

"I haven't seen my home state in a dog's age," he said.

"There you go." He meant Oklahoma, which I had never seen.

"I'd like to show you the Continental Divide, and the Corn Palace, too. This country has the grandest system of paved roads in the world. Grand is really the only word for it."

Yet he spoke like an invalid, with nostalgia. I told him I wanted him to see a doctor.

"That's impossible," he said.

It wouldn't have been impossible, but it seemed like a very great risk. HORSEFLY's name was in the papers every day. They said that the FBI was looking for him in all fifty states plus Mexico and France. Perhaps he was dead with a hole shot in his body, left somewhere to rot just as he'd fallen. I was scared of that, and we never did see a doctor.

Each day after lunch I offered Ray some bourbon. He would take a few sips. Not much. Enough to keep him calm. Or was it killing him?

I didn't know. I asked him, "Ray, what do you think? Should you have a little bit, or not?"

He'd shake his head no, then drink it.

He seemed most like himself when he sat up to smoke a cigarette. He grimaced while taking the first draw, and then he would shake the match out. He squinted through the smoke.

He talked about Stanleyville, which was something he'd never done since we left that place. He mentioned the names of men who had driven trucks for the Sheffield Beer Distributing Company. "The network went all over the east," he said. He'd had the use of a small plane as well, and a Cuban pilot who'd been assigned to him by the Agency. He mentioned many other names as though I would know them, though I didn't. Then he described some large birds which he said were shaped like human heads, and they walked up and down the road by the warehouse unmolested. "Their bodies were sort of tan-colored with a purple mark on the breast," he said. "Celeste was afraid of these birds, and so was the girl, and so was the dog."

I did not remember any such birds. Nor the dog, nor anyone named Celeste. And who was the girl?

I felt the gravity of hearing these things. A box had been pulled down from the shelf and some old items brought out and unwrapped, but not all of them. Others stayed tight in their wrappings. An idea crossed my mind which I imagine many others have thought before: These things were so neatly packed away. If we take them out, we'll never get them all back in.

Therefore, when Ray alluded to some person I didn't know, I didn't ask him to say more, and when his mind seemed to wander and he said something that didn't make sense, like that these head-shaped birds could talk, and that he had conversed with them, I let it go. Sometimes he went half to sleep, and he would talk in this state. If his dreams got very agitated I would shake him and give him a small drink.

You can see I was improvising, but it seemed to work. Soon he slept the full night through, and in the morning he sat up and said he would enjoy having some buttermilk. I went out to find some on St. Paul.

I took the back stairs out of the Fletcher. The reason was this. Henry was on day shift that day, and I was in a rush to get the buttermilk. Were

I to use the front stairs, those sad, wide-set eyes would be pulling at me. I wedged a paper match in the door lock so I could get back into the building from the alley.

If only I had not done that. Had I gone out the front, Henry would have known I was not in the room, and therefore he would not have gone up by himself when Ray started flinging things into the walls. A recluse who resided in Room 39 under the name "Sam Smith" called the desk. I had not seen his face once. He called down to Henry complaining of the disturbance from 33, and Henry, who would ordinarily have ignored such a complaint or else called the Baltimore police, came upstairs himself because he thought that Roy McJones was hurting Nurse Roberta Dewey. Had that been the case, what could the unsteady Henry have done? He was heavy and soft, and his legs were different lengths. He was no match for Ray. But he went up anyway. He knocked, and Ray got up and let him in.

It took me the better part of an hour to locate a quart of buttermilk on St. Paul. Back at Room 33, I found Ray pacing the floor in his shorts and his yellowed undershirt, kicking his bare feet through some gray fluff that was scattered over the linoleum.

I was slow to absorb the scene. The cushions from the sofa had been slashed open and emptied: that was what the gray stuff was. The folding chair was pushed over, and the hot plate was on the floor, broken open.

"What has happened?" I said.

"We're burned," Ray said.

He stepped close to me and took the paper bag from my hand. He handed me his yellow-handled sodbuster pocketknife. The single blade was opened. His arms shook as he unfolded the mouth of the buttermilk carton.

"Cover him with the knife," Ray said. He took his buttermilk into the bedroom.

I was confused. The card table was on its side in the corner, and I heard a wet cough from behind it. It was Henry. I saw his black shoe with its built-up sole. I asked Henry what he was doing behind that table.

"McJones said he would kill me," Henry said.

"What did you do to make him want to kill you?"

"Nothing!" Henry told me about the noise and Sam Smith's call.

"I need to have a word in private with Mr. McJones," I said. I backed up into the bedroom. "The desk clerk is working for us," I hissed over my shoulder to Ray.

Henry threw the flimsy card table over and rose to his knees. It was difficult to watch. He was bulky and awkward, and he was afraid.

"Mr. McJones is very sick," I said. "I'm sorry for this misunderstanding."

"Why are you lying about him?" Henry said. "Are you his daughter?"

"No! I'm not! The truth is, he's someone important—you'd understand if I told you. He needs to rest."

"He needs a drink," Henry said. "He's no different from ten other sponges in this building. They come here to die."

The brown amphibian eyes seemed to leap at me. Henry put his fist on the doorknob and rattled it, unable to make it do what he wanted. Then for some reason it opened, and he left.

Ray came out of the bedroom carrying his shoes from two fingers. The front of his shirt was wet with buttermilk. "We are burned," he said.

"That was the desk clerk!" I said.

He put a finger to my mouth to silence me. Then he came close. "You should have been more careful. He's an obvious Bureau informant. He's planted some listening device in here, and he saw you leave and came up to change the batteries. We're burned, and this phase of the thing is over." Ray dropped onto the ruined sofa and got his feet in his shoes, but he pulled one of the shoestrings into a knot. He cursed and stood up. "Idaho," he said.

"What?"

He shook his head. The ring with the Scamp keys on it hit me in the chest.

"You're sick, Ray," I said. I took his arm.

He wrenched the arm loose. Somehow I tripped on my own feet and found myself on the floor. He bent down close to me.

"Yes, I am sick. Come through for me, Jumbo. Code word Idaho."

He left. I heard his shoes clatter down the stairs, and then from the window I saw him come out from under the front awning onto the sidewalk. He caught himself on the hood of a parked green station wagon. He crossed St. Paul, and then he went away up Madison Street, gone.

27

I wanted to climb out the window and down the side of the building after him.

But I couldn't. He was sick, but Idaho meant something. I knew what it meant. Spacious, queasy-making thoughts expanded in my brain, but I pushed them down. Close, practical thoughts must be my only thoughts. I ran to get the buttermilk carton with Ray's fingerprints smeared across it. I don't know why—our fingerprints were everywhere. I dumped a hill of his cigarette butts into a paper grocery bag and pushed all my clothes into my knapsack.

There wasn't much to pack. While scanning the room, I noted a set of gouges high on the wall. It seemed that Ray had swung the hot plate into the wall by its cord, or maybe thrown it. He must have had some reason to suspect that a listening device was inside. It was a perfect hiding place—that hot plate was so filthy, we had touched it as little as possible.

I left with my arms full. At a bend in the stairs, I stopped to look for Henry. There he was in his cage, head in his hands. I climbed back up a flight and slipped out the back stairs. No paper match was needed this time, because I wouldn't be back.

Some children were wrestling at the curb near the Scamp. "Hey, chickie," one of them said to me. I got in the Scamp and cranked it, and when it lurched forward those children hopped aside.

I drove for some time, an hour or more. I don't know how. Later, when I stopped, I had no recollection of any streets I had driven through. All I seemed to be able to think of was Ray in his soaked shirt telling me to come through for him.

I had stopped alongside a parking lot. The sun was low, and the glare was such that all of the dozens of cars appeared the same steely white. I thought of something that I had seen earlier, but which hadn't registered at the time. I got my red radio out of the knapsack. The leather case had been pulled off of it and the corner of the radio crushed as though it had been stomped on. The radio could have been opened simply enough with a small screwdriver, but we didn't have one of those.

I tried turning it on—nothing.

I drove till I found a dumpster half out of sight behind a veterinarian's office. I pitched in the remains of my beloved red shortwave set. I also tossed the bag of cigarette butts and a stack of tourist brochures that I had gathered, idiotically, from a rack at Lexington Market. Time to pitch it all. Idaho was our code word meaning diverge and wait for instructions. He had told it to me on that bench in Lafayette Square, back on that Sunday when we left D.C.—the Sunday after the arrests at the Watergate. Father's Day, as a matter of fact. You can check the calendar. Idaho meant bug out, and that he said it in our code was proof that he knew what he was saying.

Could it be, really, that Henry had placed a bug in our room? The thought was ridiculous, but then in my mind the picture of him shifted, and I found I could imagine it. He'd been an easy recruitment for me. Too easy, perhaps. If a child could recruit him, why not the FBI?

For some reason I was dropping the brochures into the dumpster piece by piece, looking over them again—one for the Poe House, one for Pimlico, where I'd intended to visit. A brown envelope was in the stack, and inside the brown envelope were fourteen stiff hundred-dollar bills.

A light rain started. I drove a long, narrow street that was lined with two- and three-story rowhouses. Each house had its stack of front steps and its square of yard only big enough to hold two lawn chairs or a planter made out of a tire. I parked and locked the Scamp's doors.

The city bus stopped at the corner. A man pushed himself up the street in a wheelchair. Someone called hello to him.

Porch lights were lit, and people sat out on their steps. Windows flickered blue where television sets were on. Now and then came a laugh, a shout, or a siren. No one seemed to notice me. It was dark inside the Scamp, and I was small. Before I could sleep I seemed to sit awake on the white vinyl seat for half the night, only looking out the windows of the Scamp and thinking, thinking, thinking.

28

When I woke the air in the Scamp was stale. The windows were fogged, and my mouth and eyes were gummy. I wiped the windshield with my hand. The streetlights were still on, and the sky was a murky, sunless blue. I found an open donut shop and scrubbed my face and neck in the bathroom. The girl in the mirror appeared childish and lost, an urchin whose stringy blond locks you wouldn't like to touch.

I ate a donut, and it was good. Let me say that again. I like a plain cake donut, no glaze, no sprinkles. Other things went out of my head while I ate this donut. The outside was crisp and toasty with a tallowy aroma and hints of nutmeg. The yellow interior was soft and dense. I stood in line for a second one and enjoyed it almost as much. The name of this shop was Mister Donut.

In the middle of eating my second donut an observation came that struck me as so important, I almost wrote it down. I didn't, for security reasons, but I have kept it nearby in my mind. The observation was that, the night before, in the Scamp, I had nearly despaired. I had wanted to ball up and hide, a useless feeling from which nothing good can ever come. And I'd made a bad decision, sleeping in the car on a neighborhood street. Any police officer knocking on the glass could have ruined everything for me and Ray. It was time for me to rise to the business at hand.

I needed to get out of Baltimore. Philadelphia was not a far drive. I also needed to make a call to the classified department at the Sarasota offices of the *World News Digest.* I would put in a signal to Ray to tell him that I was safe and awaiting instructions.

I went into the glove compartment for a map and pulled out a slip of paper I didn't recognize. It was a carbon from a restaurant ticket. The figure $200 was on there twice in ballpoint. That didn't sound like any meal that Ray or I would have ordered. There were other pen scratches I couldn't read. It was Chinese: the receipt for our Tennessee driver's licenses. They were to have been ready today. We had forgotten.

I had two donuts in me now and intended to do the smart thing, as soon as I figured out what that was. Here was my first thought: a driver's license would be awfully useful to me. It was already half paid for, and also, the licenses had our pictures on them. I remembered those melancholy faces spread out on the desktop, and I did not want ours to be among them.

Here was the other side of it. Idaho meant *bug out*, not *leave and come back the next morning*. Why have a plan if you're not going to follow it?

I thought it over for a long time.

A black bird walked on its stick legs in the Mister Donut parking lot. Three cars arrived together, and the bird jumped up and shot away. The day was beginning. The people who had slept in beds were coming out for breakfast and to see what was going on. It was time for me to move, time to grow up, time to do the next thing.

made my call to Sarasota, then went to Sears and Roebuck. I was there when they unlocked the doors. In the dressing room I pulled on a set of magenta Toughskins with stiff reinforcing patches on the insides of the knees. I added a plaid shirt, and my hair went up in a golf cap with a medallion on the peak. It was that or a football helmet.

I drove to the alley behind Lucky Bus Tour. Spicy smoke crept out the rear door of the Golden Monkey Restaurant, along with clatters and shouts. The door was propped open with a chair. I'd been watching for two minutes, waiting for I don't know what, when the simple-minded Chinese girl hauled a bucket out and eyed me dully.

She emptied her bucket of kitchen scraps into the garbage. Idly I wondered what she could possibly be throwing out. It was my understanding that the Chinese chefs used everything, down to and including the claws.

When she'd gone I walked the twenty steps to the rear door of Lucky Bus Tour. My knock was answered by the man with the tassel beard. I had interrupted his lunch. He held the door open with the toe of his slipper and continued slurping noodles while he peered at me. I showed the receipt, then removed the golf cap. He let me in.

"Two hundred dollars," he said.

"Let's see what you've done."

He brought two cards from the desk drawer. The picture of Ray gave me pause. I didn't dwell on it just then, however.

"So, you are nineteen," he said. "If you ever need some work, let me know. Great pay, short hours."

"I will need that receipt back plus the original," I said.

"What original?"

I was reminding him how carbons work when a bell dinged up

front, followed by a shout in Chinese. I followed him up the corridor. Another Chinese man grabbed his arm. Out in the street, through the glass, I saw the simpleminded girl run past silently, black braids flying.

The two men hadn't seen her. They exited to the left, leaving me by myself.

I went back and opened the top drawer of the desk. The original of my receipt was there on top of the pad. Simple enough. I tore it out, the carbon paper as well, and folded them in my pocket. I couldn't help noticing half a dozen U.S. passports also in the drawer. One had belonged to a woman born in 1956. I was tempted to help myself to it but didn't. It would be stealing. A person need not become a criminal, just because she is being hunted by the FBI. I laid two hundreds in the drawer, pushed my hair up into the cap again, and went out the way I'd come in.

Because the alley was one-way, I had to go out the other end and wound up driving the Scamp back in front of the Golden Monkey Restaurant. It appeared the whole restaurant had emptied into the sidewalk and street. At the center of the commotion Mr. Wang, the cauliflower-cheeked man, held his hand up wrapped in a towel. The front of his shirt had a goodly amount of blood on it, I mean about the amount you would get from a few long squirts of a squeeze-type mustard container. Not a life-ending amount of blood, but more than you want to see. He was crying. His gray-haired mother darted about inside the crowd, brandishing a long cleaver and shrieking at a birdlike pitch. The cleaver blade was a dark, heavy-looking chunk of steel that would have been well suited for severing pigs' joints or even taking down a small tree. I eased the Scamp by. Mother Wang met my eyes and seemed to tilt the blade at me.

I had put two blocks behind me before I looked again at the picture on Ray's license. I was distressed because he looked awful in it. He hadn't shaved, and that softness on his jaw which I'd hardly noticed in person made him appear haggard in the small portrait. Worse than haggard. His hair was a fringe across his forehead, and his neck wasn't straight. The gaze coming out from under the eyebrows was wary and dark.

I had watched him stand for that picture, but I hadn't really *seen* him. He'd been sick for some time, and now he was sick and alone.

That was a low moment, when I was looking at his picture in the Scamp.

I had to remind myself that I was driving. I checked my hands on the wheel—ten and two—and I checked my speed. I raised my hand to the rearview mirror to adjust it. There in the back seat, looking back at me in the mirror, was the simpleminded Chinese girl.

about jumped out of my Toughskins. I whipped the Scamp to the curb. There she was, skinny as a pup and looking very worried, but stationary.

"Get out, Chinese," I said.

She twisted to look out the back window.

"Out of my car now!" I said.

She slid down in the seat, then farther down, so I couldn't see her.

I went around to the back passenger door. The slow girl was knotted up on the floor, showing only her backside and the red rubber soles of her shoes. I got my hands around one hard brown ankle, but I might as well have been trying to pull a boxwood shrub out of the ground.

A lady police officer came to stand beside me. "Is something the matter here?" she said.

"Of course not."

"You are parked in front of my fire hydrant."

It was true. I had even banged my leg on her fire hydrant while pulling the Chinese girl's ankle.

"I'll move the car," I said.

"You'll move it after I write you a ticket." The lady police officer flipped open her pad and clicked a pen.

"Please don't."

"Sorry, Charlie." She took a step backward and sideways to see the tag.

That wouldn't do. I snatched the pen from her fingers and threw it as hard as I could down the sidewalk.

She hadn't expected that. Quickly I got behind the wheel of the Scamp again. I snatched it into drive and kicked the accelerator, and we shot through a red light, just missing a Honda motorcycle.

I had memorized my route out of town. The farther this Chinese girl rode with me, however, the farther I would be traceable. The thing to do was to pin five dollars to her shirt and call her a cab, if I could only extract her from the back seat.

I saw her face in the mirror again. She wasn't a kid. She might have been twenty-five, though it was hard to tell. "Why are you in my car?" I asked.

"Wang mother try to *keyhole* me," she said.

The way she spoke was strangely effortful, as though the words were objects to be removed from her mouth. "I don't know what that means," I said.

"You don't know what *keyhole* somebody mean? Chop somebody with cleaver knife so she will die?" She made a slashing gesture.

In the mirror I studied her hard, dark eyes. I got what she was saying now, and I got something else, too. She wasn't simpleminded.

interrogated her as follows.

ME: Why did Wang's mother want to kill you?

CHINESE: Because I have chop Wang finger.

ME: Why have you chopped Wang's finger?

CHINESE: I have chop vegetable. [She pronounced the word with its full four syllables: *vedge uh tuh bow*.] He have grope and fondle.

ME: Fondling you?

CHINESE: Yes!

ME: You like Wang?

CHINESE: Like?

ME: [I made a two-handed signal.] You and Wang.

CHINESE: No! Oh, no, no, no, no, no. Wang? [She said a hundred words in her own language.]

ME: So when he groped you, you chopped his finger off?

CHINESE: No, I ignore and keep on chop.

ME: You're saying it was an accident, then.

CHINESE: Accident. Mother come in, Wang jump, I am chop his finger!

ME: Okay. Very good! Now the police will be after you and me both.

CHINESE: Nope. No police. Mother will *keyhole*!

ME: Where do you want me to drop you?

CHINESE: Drop me?

ME: Have you got some family in town?

CHINESE: In Taiwan.

ME: Got your passport?

CHINESE: Wang have passport.

ME: In that case you have no choice but to go back to Wang. You can't do anything without your passport.

CHINESE: Where is you father?

ME: What do you know about my father?

CHINESE: Maybe you father need ID like me.

ME: Get out of my car. No. Don't get out. Why did you say that?

CHINESE: Maybe, I think Wang have make false ID for you.

ME: What do you mean, maybe you think?

CHINESE: I have see these ID card. You are too small to drive. How old?

ME: Nineteen.

CHINESE: I think fourteen, maybe less. You have too small chin. That will still grow some more. You have little neck. Mm. Tell me, where is you father?

ME: My father got those ID cards as a joke, that's all. A practical joke.

CHINESE: What is "practical joke"?

ME: That's a gag you pull around the office. Little tricks you play on your friends.

CHINESE: Trick you friends, good idea. Why will you need false card too?

ME: I'm part of the joke.

CHINESE: Where are you going to right now?

ME: Philadelphia. Look here. I will give you fifty dollars if you will get out of my car and don't tell a soul that you've seen me.

CHINESE: Fifty? Your father has paid four hundred dollar to play some funny joke on his friends.

ME: I will give you fifty.

She gave a small, quick nod. I pulled a bill from the brown envelope.

ME: Have you got change for a hundred?

CHINESE: No.

ME: I will give you one hundred, then. You are a cunning Chinese, aren't you? Now you've got to forget everything we've talked about.

CHINESE: It never make sense anyway.

I looked her over good. She had on plain black slacks, the black cloth slippers with red rubber soles, and a white double-knit top with long points on the collar. There was a grease spot on the blouse, below her ribs. I have already mentioned that her coarse black hair was in two tight braids.

ME: Goodbye.

CHINESE: Only, I think you should drop me in Philadelphia.

ME: Are you serious?

CHINESE: Mm.

ME: What are you going to do in Philadelphia?

CHINESE: You don't have to think about it.

ME: I'm not a taxi service. You've got money—you can take the train to Philadelphia. Or New York. They've got a great big Chinatown full of your people.

CHINESE: Can't go to Chinatown. Wang will find me there, somebody will send me back to Baltimore, and Wang mother will have me keyhole or break leg, chop off finger, something. Maybe your funny father need a housekeeper.

ME: He won't like your references.

32

I drove out the north edge of Baltimore into Harford County, spinning a new cover story as I went. To rule out any notion that Ray might take her in on charity, as the Wangs had done, I described a prisonlike boarding school to which I must return this very afternoon. The girl bunking over me had a strong odor. I hardly knew what I would say until I heard myself say it. It is exactly how one should never build a cover.

The Chinese asked me to describe the girl's smell further.

"Like Comet," I said. "She has purple bags under both eyes, too."

"What is Comet?"

"A powder for cleaning sinks."

The Chinese considered. "She might have some parasite. Could be anything."

I laid on some business about what a miserable life it was, shut up in a dormitory with all the other odd girls, mostly petty thieves, who'd been sent away from their homes.

"You should not complain. Father spend all that money to have you educate."

"School's for suckers," I blathered.

"You are a bad daughter."

It stung me! That's a queer side effect of putting some energy into your lie.

We had come some miles out of the city when the Chinese blurted, "Stop car." She got out and walked toward some trees, then doubled over, carsick. She came back and knelt at the window. I asked her was she done.

"Done throw up," she said.

I passed her a box of Chiclets. She stared at a blue one on her wrinkled palm until I told her to put it in her mouth.

She did so, then tipped her head to one side, like a highly intelligent dog will do. She chewed the blue Chiclet twice, then spun away to spit it where the beer and Sprite cans, potato chip bags, and other trash lay along the greasy, gravelly edge of the road. She stood awhile with her shoulders curved, fingertips pressed to the top of her nose. Then she got back into the Scamp.

"Take me someplace that have cigarette," she said.

That was easy. From the glove compartment I gave her a nearly full pack of Raleighs with a matchbook tucked down under the cellophane. To light the match she held it stationary and struck the book against it, instead of the reverse, as every other person I have ever seen strike a match has done.

"I will stay here," she said. She got out of the car.

Was it that easy? I wished I had thought to ply her with cigarettes earlier. "I don't mind driving you to a bus station," I said.

She wagged her thumb.

"Fine," I said. Hitchhiking is risky for most girls, but in light of Wang's finger I was more concerned for whoever picked her up.

I tossed the pack of Raleighs out the window to her. It flipped through the air until she clapped her small, neat hands together on it.

I left her standing in the high grass beside the road.

33

It was a relief to have the scowling Asian out of my Scamp. I crossed a bridge over a reservoir, and she was history. With no passport her prospects were bad, but there is a saying, *No es mi problema.* Anyway I'd left her a hundred smackers ahead.

For some reason I turned to look at the back seat, where she'd been. There on the white vinyl was Benjamin Franklin, about to slide down the crack. The sly Chinese had left my gift behind. Was this some special Far Eastern brand of insult? Or was it a way to free her conscience?

Well, I didn't want her conscience freed. I had bought that Chinese waitress, and I meant for her to stay bought. But when I got back over the bridge to the spot where I had left her, she was gone. No traffic had passed, so I took the hundred with me down a wide trail into the woods, calling, "Hey! Chinese girl!"

I emerged at the edge of the reservoir. On the narrow gray beach, on the moss of a fallen tree trunk, I found Ray's pack of Raleighs.

I looked all around me for a long time. No Chinese girl. But then I did see her, or only her head, ten yards out in the water with the sun on it, one hand up with a cigarette between the fingers.

"What in the heck are you doing out there?"

"Smoke cigarette! Go away!"

"Go away? This is weird! Where are your clothes?"

"I have them."

"You have them?"

She put the cigarette in her mouth, and I saw her shirt cuff. She was wearing her shirt.

"This is a new extreme of modesty," I said. "You are bathing alone in a deserted lake in the woods in all of your clothes." I looked again and saw the marks of her rubber-soled slippers leading into the water. What about that? She had her shoes on, too.

"Why have you come here? Go."

"I came to bring you this money back." I shook the bill.

"Don't want it!"

"You will need it," I said. "Also, you do want it. You bargained with me for it."

After a silent half minute she said, "Leave it on the tree."

"When I bribe somebody, I mean for her to stay bribed!"

"Leave on tree!"

"It will blow away."

"Put a rock on top!"

"I am not leaving this one-hundred-dollar bill on a tree trunk with a rock on it. Suppose you were to drown out there! Can you swim, Chinese? What are you doing, standing on the bottom of the lake? I never heard of somebody smoking a cigarette while swimming. Is that how you do it in Taiwan?"

The head came closer. That was creepy to see. She had taken her braids out, and the wet hair clung to her neck like seaweed. She rose toward the shore in *Creature from the Black Lagoon* fashion, dark water streaming. The heavy pants pulled at her hips. She pinched the cigarette in her mouth and scooped handfuls of gray sand from both her pants pockets.

"Why do you have sand in your pockets?"

She only scowled at me and wouldn't answer.

"Turn them inside out," I suggested.

But the pockets weren't lined, so they couldn't be turned inside out. She kept scooping.

"You are an odd thing," I said.

"Always go swim with sand in my pockets. Make the lungs work."

"Now your clothes are soaking wet and your pockets have sand in them, nut job."

Something burst out of her mouth. I first thought it was a sneeze, but no, it was her language. She went off on a long, mad tear of mush-like syllables, knee-deep in the murky reservoir. She turned her back and worked her arms. Heaven knows what she was saying. It might have been classical Confucian mottoes, or there again, it might have been a Chinese form of gibberish. It seems natural to me that a Chinese person's gibberish would also sound Chinese, just like Tintin's dog when he barks sounds Belgian. "*Wooah wooah!*"

When the thing was done being said, whatever it was, she waded up to the beach and snatched the hundred from my grip. She pushed the stiff bill into her wet, sandy pants pocket. "Now can go shopping!"

"Excuse me. What have I done?"

She glowered. For her it wasn't enough to be an obstacle impeding my progress: she had to be unpleasant as well.

34

That morning at Sears and Roebuck I had bought myself a patchwork print dress in yellow, red, and brown with a short skirt, puffy sleeves, and a green collar. I allowed the Chinese girl to put it on. It fit her all right. She was only a little taller than I and somewhat fuller through the hips. She wouldn't tell her age.

I drove west. "I bet you are hungry," I said. "Swimming always makes me hungry." I found the highway and stopped at a Stuckey's. She didn't know what to order, so I got us two BLTs. She took hers apart and devoured the bacon first. Then she ate the pickle spear and a parsley sprig that probably had not been washed, since it was a garnish and not meant to be eaten. Then she ate the lettuce, after using a butter knife to scrape the mayonnaise off.

The tabletop was made of white Formica with glitter in it and a dull band of aluminum around the edge. The Chinese girl rubbed her finger on the Formica as though trying to determine how the glitter was stuck on. She handled everything: the bottle of ketchup with its grimy white cap, the chrome napkin dispenser, the stamped-metal ashtray, and the bowl made of lacquered wood chips that held the sugar packets.

"Anyway, what is your name?" I said.

"*Baydee.*"

"Baydee?"

"*Baydee.* Like *Baydee Graybo.*"

"Betty?"

"Yeah. *Baydee.*"

She knocked a blob of ketchup onto her plate and dipped the edge of a tomato slice in it. Her bites were small and cautious, but she chewed fast.

A woman followed me into the ladies' room and asked where I was from.

"I only meant it making conversation," she said when I didn't answer. "Fran and I left Augusta at daylight, and I'm so bored I could scream!" Fran was her husband. He made a habit of driving under the speed limit because he believed it to be easier on the vehicle. "But it is harder on the wife," she said. "I would rather put the wear on the Oldsmobile than spend one extra minute shut inside it not allowed to remark on things I notice." She asked where my parents were.

"Home."

"You don't mean to tell me you are traveling alone!"

I told her I was traveling with my chaperone. Just then Betty came in and began flushing out her mouth with water noisily.

The woman from Augusta pressed the heels of her blue patent-leather shoes together, waiting for the sink. Betty dried off neatly with a single paper towel and left without having said a word or looking once at either of us.

"I would not like to have an Oriental chaperone," the woman from Augusta said.

"Tell me why you won't go to Chinatown," I said to Betty when we were back in the Scamp.

"Wang will find me there."

"Is Wang the one who brought you from Taiwan?"

"Wang and some other. They have arrange for me to come to U.S., but I have to work here to pay. Work me like a donkey because I have not got any paper. I will be an old woman broke to pieces when I pay that money."

She was smoking another Raleigh now, tapping the ash at the top of the window.

She saw me looking at her and looked back awhile. I had to look away first, since I was driving.

"You get some makeup, you can maybe look more grown," she said. "Change your hair. When you push this hair behind your ear, like this"—she touched the spot on my head with her finger—"that make you look like a little girl. You can maybe part your hair on this side and pull it back away from *forehead*. Make you look older. Get some older-looking shoes, too. You have one of this?" She smacked her chest with both hands.

"I have two of that."

"I mean garment. What you wear here."

"A brassiere?"

"If you will get brassiere and maybe put two small towel in it. Your bottom too small, too. Maybe you can put on seven eight underwear, make you bottom seem more big."

"Mm."

"You can sew?"

"Anybody can sew a little bit."

"No. I will maybe sew you some pad for your hips. Give you some big hips, not so straight like a pencil. You never will fool somebody that have some sense, but most people don't have any sense. You will be surprise. That is how I live, by so many people don't have sense."

I asked to know what she meant by that.

"People supposed to have paper to live here. I don't have paper. Supposed to give tax. I don't give tax. Work for cash. In Golden Monkey, many time people will buy food and will not eat. Come for lunch, buy two bowl, eat one bowl and say throw that other bowl out. I will eat it. Look at me, I don't have money but I am so fat." She held up her arm and slapped at the upper part with her hand. It was not fat by any means, but she was healthy enough. "I eat meat, vegetable, anything. People have so easy life, nobody really show maybe very much attention. I find some money on the sidewalk. I will eat better from throw away food than some powerful Chinese official will eat. Nobody starve in this country. In China if not for starve we have a lot more people. In all of Chinese history, lot of starve."

Abruptly she leaned forward and switched on the radio.

35

The Philadelphia boarding school evaporated. It just went away. I'd been outplayed and did not rush to replace my first cockamamie tall tale with a second.

I drove for hours, waiting for an idea to enter my head. I didn't know where to go. Betty became alert once when we passed a pig farm, and once again when I tried to pass a milk truck on a curve. Otherwise she maintained a half-napping state. If she needed something, she told me. "I am thirsty," she would announce. I'd pull over and get her a Coke, and then she'd be silent for another forty-five minutes.

At last I had to stop. I chose a place called the King's Way Motor Court—eight cinder-block cottages all facing different directions. The rate was nine dollars a night.

Cottage 6 at the King's Way made the room at the Fletcher seem downright well appointed. There was one tiny bed, not even a true single, and a rollaway folded by the wall. Betty took one look and said she was going for a walk. I was tired from driving and thought, Maybe she won't come back.

But she did. I was lying on top of the sheet, having stripped the dusty bedspread off. She stood in the doorway, looking.

I got up to help her unfold the rollaway. When we lowered the two halves, a reek of must and ammonia rolled out. Some hundred or so flat insects teemed over the blue and tan ticking.

Betty let out a groan, and for my own part, I nearly vomited. The bugs were little black things running here and there. We closed the bed and shoved it out the door at a run. The rolling bed cleared two concrete steps before coming to rest on all four wheels.

Betty wanted to have it out with the management, but I reminded her she was on the lam from Wang. "Don't give a clerk a reason to remember you." This would be my tactic again in days to come. When-ever we needed to practice clandestinity, which was almost all the time, I would tell Betty it was for her sake.

We bunked together in the miniature single bed. The sentence that kept running through my brain was, There is a Chinese in the bed with me.

I tried not to think about Ray. No one was looking after him now, but indulging my worries and fears would not help me to deserve the confi-dence he had placed in me.

36

I awoke and sat up, remembering where I was. The Chinese was gone. From the window I saw that the Scamp was still there.

I pulled on my tunic dress and walked to a concrete picnic table at the far end of the parking lot. One end of the table was under a mulberry branch, and the berries had made purple stains on it.

Way in the distance, there was my yellow, red, and brown patchwork print dress walking toward me with Betty inside it. Her tawny arms and legs became distinct. I'd been thinking about this Chinese lady-girl and how strange it was, her stowing away in my car just after we'd cut Henry loose. The dress had pockets on the sides, and before she sat she emptied them of five or six plums.

"How's your handler?" I said.

"My what?"

"The case officer you just now reported to."

I watched her neck and face for color. No change. She unfolded a paper napkin and rubbed at the skin of a plum.

"I'm talking about your spymaster," I said.

"You think I will spy on you?" She gave me the plum and began polishing another.

"Could be!"

"You are right. Your boarding school teacher are very worry, girl. They tell me watch out for you."

"Is that so?"

"Sure. They say, 'Make that girl eat a lot of plum. Too skinny.'"

She touched one of her eyes as though to get something out of it. She blinked a couple of times.

This followed.

ME: It's time for you to come clean.
BETTY: What do you mean, come clean?

ME: I know you don't work for my boarding school, because I made it up. Tell me the truth.

BETTY: I come from mainland.

ME: What?

BETTY: Not from Taiwan.

ME: You mean to tell me you come from Red China?

BETTY: [She glared at me.]

ME: How did you wind up in Baltimore?

BETTY: Complicated.

ME: Tell it!

BETTY: Wang's people bring me here from Hong Kong.

ME: Do they know you are from the mainland?

BETTY: Yeah. Can't lie about that.

ME: You lied to me about it.

BETTY: You are not Chinese. For me to lie to Chinese, that will be like you say you are from Texas. Any white people can tell you are not from Texas, right? Chinese people, if they are been around, can maybe tell I am from Peking. Wang have travel around and he can tell. So he will have that on my head all the time.

ME: Who has your passport?

BETTY: Real one is gone. I will never get that.

ME: How did you escape Red China without it?

BETTY: A man have it. It is complicated.

ME: I can see it is complicated. Tell me all of it, and make it the true version this time, or I will report you to some people who will make Mr. Wang and his mother look like the Neighborhood Welcome Committee.

BETTY: I have travel with Chinese table tennis team. I was a translator.

ME: I hope you were the second string.

BETTY: What string? I don't know what you are talking about.

ME: Your English is not so good.

BETTY: I know! I should not go, but someone have make me go!

ME: Settle down. When you get warmed up like that, I can't understand what you're saying. Just tell me the truth, all right?

BETTY: You beat my brow too much.

ME: Go on and tell it.

BETTY: I have had adult relationship with one party official who will travel with table tennis players. He has preferred me as his translator because we were a special friend. This is true. I tell him, I don't like to translate, I might make a bad impression or maybe will get some word wrong. But he will like to travel with me. I cannot say more because I am ashame.

ME: You are talking about a sexual entanglement.

BETTY: [She nodded once with a look like she had bitten a lime.]

ME: I don't need to know each detail of that part. This party official brought you to Hong Kong as his special friend. Then what?

BETTY: Then we have a bad fight. I tell him again, I do not like this way. I am ashame. He have family. People know and are discuss me. I am look down. For me it is bad. I was a good student. I have work very hard on the farm, but I study school, go to Peking University. Very good university. Study English. I think I will learn to speak English very well. I have copy and recite many hours every day. Don't want to go back to farm. Mm. I become involve with this man—one stupid mistake. Then, in Hong Kong he said something that has made me feel very angry. I ran out. I could not go back then. Two stupid mistake. I am now like a dead person. Maybe it is as though I have jump off a bridge. Can't jump back up. Even if I will have a passport, it will be no good. I am out of this world. Like a wild animal, no home, no name, no connection to anyone. Like a snake living alone inside a narrow hole. Just quiet all the time, don't tell anybody anything, don't have someone to tell something to. I am glad I told you. If you tell someone this I will get send back to People's Republic of China, maybe put on prison farm to work all my life. I am no good to my country anymore. Very sad, let people down for be licentious. I am sad.

Now her neck was red and she cried awhile. She cried like she ate, in many small bites. It went on until she lit a Raleigh.

ME: Your situation is not so bad. Refugees from Communist nations often seek U.S. asylum.

BETTY: I don't want U.S. asylum. I am not a refugee. I am a revolutionary!

found I could not stop staring at this wiry brown creature. I don't think I can describe the uneasy feeling it gave me. It was bedbugs all over again, only this time it was bedbugs of the mind.

She was not just the enemy but the pure stock, straight out of Peking! And yet here she was, a helpless mess, negligible in size, with plum on her mouth, in tears.

They were the confused tears of a Communist. I reminded myself of this. The hard little fists in front of me on the concrete were like the hard paws of a fox or coyote. She was a vicious pack animal, too small to do much killing by herself, but able to bite and scratch and do serious harm.

"You must feel very lost," I said. "I imagine life is different here, compared to Peking, China."

"Mm. Yes."

A minor breeze caused the branch at the end of the picnic table to lose a long mulberry. It rolled an inch on the concrete surface. There were ants on the table, too, walking in curves, and a beetlelike insect, and gray lichen, and bits of twig.

"The people of my country won't hurt you," I said. "Foreigners from every nation have come to America to make a new home. Even your Communist belief system, while not welcome here, is not illegal."

She let out a long breath. Resignation was one way to read it.

I suggested she would feel happier if she told me her Chinese name. She did, but then I couldn't repeat it to her satisfaction. My mouth wouldn't form those sounds.

"Better if you keep call me Betty," she said. "The other name is finish."

"Okay, Betty. Look here. We have made some solid progress just now. Let me point something out to you." I bit into the plum she'd wiped for me. "We have both caught each other out now, Betty. Do you see what I mean?"

"No."

"I told you a tall tale, and you told me a tall tale. Then each of us caught the other out. That means you've got my number, and I've got yours. Do you see? We're *involved*. We may as well trust each other. But sometimes, Betty, it is hard for me to guess what you are thinking."

"What I am thinking is pretty simple," she said. "Can easily guess."

"Are you hating America? Are you hating me?"

"No! You say you are try to help me!"

That took me back, because I did not remember saying it. But of course I *had* said it—only I hadn't expected her to believe me. Perhaps she was worse off than I had guessed. Putting it in the agent recruitment terms I had learned from Ray, the problem in Betty's case wasn't *finding* a vulnerability but *choosing* one.

"I will help you if you will trust me," I said.

"Have no choice but trust you," she said.

38

"I have a friend who may be able to get you papers," I said. "But you must promise to say nothing about my father."

I never had given Betty a viable cover story to replace the stinker about the boarding school. She was a lot of work to lie to. Most people will meet you halfway for a lie, helping you out with an "I see what you mean," "That has happened to me, too," or the like. But Betty, when she wasn't angry or crying, mostly wore a Mount Rushmore–type expression.

We drove to West Virginia. The trip took us past Harpers Ferry, and I debated whether to point it out. What thoughts would it give rise to inside the skull of a Maoist? I wound up telling her a two-minute version of John Brown's raid on the Federal arsenal. She took it in. "America is very racist," she opined.

Here is the other small highlight of the trip. I said, "Keep your eye out for a yellow post," for that was the marker for the private road onto which we would turn. Minutes went by, and I said aloud, "Where is that yellow post?"

"Way back," Betty said.

She had *watched* for it and *seen* it, but she hadn't bothered to *mention* it.

I turned the Scamp around. I said, "You are strange to me, Betty. I don't understand you a bit. You claim to come from China, but I wonder if you are from space."

We drove a tenth of a mile through the woods. The driveway had a quiltlike topping of loose, clean gravel on it. Otherwise, the place had not changed much in the couple of years since I had spent a Christmas break here. The house was long and low, with a lot of roof, and in the yard there were corncobs on poles for the squirrels. Out back was a steel barn with a paddock beside it.

The moment of making the introductions would be crucial. I

needed to set the terms, and the only way to do that is by speaking first, face-on, with your hands out of your pockets and ready to snatch the advantage. This is called "dominating the situation."

I thought I had caught a break when I saw Betty's head tip forward. The music of the gravel under our tires had lulled her to sleep, I supposed. I ran and punched the doorbell, and Alex Gandy opened the door.

The sight of Ray's best friend's head could be startling, even when you knew what to expect. His head was like a short log, bulky and rough down the sides. His coarse silver hair had been allowed to grow bushy since retirement, and the woolly sideburns were also new. He wore jeans, brown socks, and a clean, unpressed cotton shirt.

"Sorry not to have called. Ray's out of pocket, and I've got a Chinese Maoist asleep in the car."

There was a kind of frown that Alex Gandy often used, a vague, downturned smile with a friendly wonderment behind it. He seemed to ask himself, What small thing has gone wrong that I can fix?

I saw his eyes fasten on to something just past my shoulder. I twisted. There was Betty, at my side. The little Asian Boris Karloff had followed right behind me.

"There you are, Betty. Betty, this is my friend Mr. Howell. Mr. Howell, I was just now telling Betty that you have often told me, 'Roberta, drop in whenever you're in West Virginia.' So here we are, Roberta and Betty, dropping in on Mr. Howell." I was winking my right eye, not my good eye for winking, but I had Betty on the left.

Mr. Gandy took in a long breath. "Betty, I'm so glad to meet you," he said. "I was on my way to the barn to see Mrs. Howell. Shall we walk out together?"

A large gray poodle pressed its nose against Betty. Betty had not been moving noticeably, and yet she became somehow even more motionless now, with the poodle's nose upon her. Mr. Gandy, seeing the problem, sent the dog inside.

The barn boots were kept on the porch in a row. Mr. Gandy turned one upside down and gave it a knock.

"Once I found a black widow spider in my boot," he said, smiling.

Betty looked like a cat on a leash: feet apart, back curled, waiting to have her neck pulled.

39

Mr. Gandy entered the barn alone. I wonder what was said in there. Minutes passed before he appeared again, following Mrs. Gandy, who came at me with both arms out, but only to grab my hands and squeeze them once. "I'm so glad you've come!" she said. She was a tall woman with a lean, strong figure and a queenly manner. Her hair was colored blond to mask the gray. She pivoted silently to Betty, ready to be introduced. That was her way of dominating the situation.

In no time she had Betty in the saddle on a sleepy black mare with a drooping lower lip. The mare was called Babe. I had ridden her myself. Betty sat very straight and solemn upon Babe with the skirt of my patchwork print dress bunched up around her thighs and the reins in both hands as Mrs. Gandy led the horse in a circle. Mr. Gandy and I stood under a walnut tree. I stepped on a wet walnut husk, and some of the black liquid got on my shoe.

"Where is Ray?" Mr. Gandy said.

"Before we get to that, please listen. That Chinese is a Communist from the mainland! She's an illegal but might be of use."

"Of use to whom?"

"To our government. She claims to have party connections inside Red China." I told him Betty's story about the ping-pongers and her party official boyfriend.

"Is this a joke? Are you listening, Ray?" He seemed to peer into my hair.

"No, no. This is real. I'm convinced she is a straight-up-and-down Maoist. I get that feeling because of a number of things which it's difficult to put my finger on. She's not like you and me. Spend a few minutes with her. Three months ago she was riding her bicycle around Peking, munching fried crickets."

"Where in the heck did you get her?"

"We met her in a restaurant."

"Where is Ray?"

I told Mr. Gandy that I would very much like to tell him that information, but first he would have to agree to keep it in the strictest confidence, including from Agency friends.

"I can't agree to keep that kind of confidence."

"This is coming straight from Ray, Mr. Gandy. Ray made me promise. I can't tell you anything except on the condition you keep it secret."

"All right. Agreed."

"Ray's in love," I said.

"What?"

"He has fallen in love with a widow named Edel. They're traveling in New Mexico, with my blessing."

"He left you alone to go on a trip with his girlfriend?"

"That's right. She's been giving me piano lessons."

"What are you, Angela, fourteen?"

"Sixteen," I lied. "I just received my driver's license."

Checks of light moved on his loglike head as the walnut leaves above us were jostled by air. "Why did you bring that Chinese girl here?"

"It was Ray's idea."

"What am I supposed to do with her?"

"Contact the Agency. Get her to a safe house. She's got no passport—that's her first vulnerability. She won't trust any Chinese, because she's on the run from this fellow Wang who imported her. She will make a useful asset for our side."

"She might make a useful asset if she were in China," Mr. Gandy said. "Where can I call Ray?"

"Mm. They're in the desert. Camping under the stars."

"What is the woman's name? Odle?"

"Edel."

"First name?"

"Gloria. Not to press the point, but did you happen to mention to Mrs. Gandy that I am going by the name of Roberta with this Chinese?"

"I mentioned it," he said. He sniffed. "Don't worry about Marie. She seldom forgets an alias."

40

From the barn came a hard knocking, accompanied by an awful nonhuman squeal. Mrs. Gandy ran for the barn while Mr. Gandy held the black mare's head. I ran after Mrs. Gandy. The skinny red gelding was in there alone, weaving his head over the stall door and blowing air.

"Red wants part of the action," Mrs. Gandy said.

"I will ride him," I said.

"No, you won't." She got him out of the stall and put him in cross-ties in the barn aisle. She showed me the spray of crescent-shaped dents where he'd kicked the back of his stall. "He's too nervous and flaky for an inexperienced rider."

"I remember that about him," I said. I at least wanted credit for having paid attention.

When she had the horse secured she turned to me. "Where is Ray and why are you here without him?"

I went through my love-in-the-desert story again.

She received it more or less like a dirty handkerchief. The question was not whether to use it, but how to dispose of it.

"I'm going to let Alex deal with that," she said. "For now, you are here, and this horse needs brushing."

I guess he had rolled in some mud, because I raised a good cloud of dust using the brush on his back. I loved that work. When I had finished, Mrs. Gandy showed me how to clean his feet.

It's a curious thing, holding a horse's foot. The foot hangs heavy and loose from its backward ankle. I worked the pick through the hollow alongside the part that is called the frog, releasing some clay and a small gray stone. I set the foot down, and the horse shifted several hundred pounds of weight onto it. He sighed.

"Some care is all he wanted," Mrs. Gandy said.

It was hard for me to imagine not being content inside that barn. The dusty, shady orderliness and the sweet smell of hay appealed to me. There was a black and white cat in the hayloft, sitting up straight with his eyes closed. Everything and everyone had a place.

When we let Red out, Betty was where we had left her, astride the droopy-lipped mare. Babe's lips had gray fuzz on them and a few long hairs like whiskers. I put my hand on her mouth. The soft lips groped at my fingers.

Betty was unhappy. "Want to get down."

"Come on down, then," I said.

Betty swung her right leg over the animal's head. Now she was sitting sideways on the horse, as though it were a park bench. Her face wore an empty look as she slid down from the saddle, landing square on both her Chinese slippers.

"That's one way to do it," Mr. Gandy said.

"I'll get on now," I said.

Mr. Gandy laced his fingers and launched me up, and Babe and I followed Mrs. Gandy and Red down a soft track at the edge of the woods. We gave Betty and Mr. Gandy some time in which to puzzle each other out. For a while, I forgot my Betty-related cares.

The world does look altogether more manageable from the back of a horse. Babe had an easy walk. Soft gnats were bumping around next to our bodies, and her smooth sides were warm. I liked being aloft on her back, rocking up and down, spotting rabbits and approving of them as though I were a prince and owned it all.

41

Later Mrs. Gandy butchered a melon for us, and I watched a hungry Betty eat right down through the flesh and into the white part of the rind, almost to the skin. I don't know whether that is the Chinese way of eating a melon or only Betty's way.

Mr. Gandy said he would cook us a fresh chicken. I'd seen their little flock sorting the edges of the manure pile. "The freshly killed farm chicken is not like the store-bought chicken," Mr. Gandy said.

Betty nodded. "More delicious."

Gandy liked that. "She knows!" He attempted to clap a large basket down over a brown hen, but the bird kept getting away. He started toward the house for his .22 rifle, but Mrs. Gandy forbade it. Not around the horses.

"We'll have steaks," Mr. Gandy said. He set them frozen on a hot grill. Mine was all right. Betty was astonished at the size of the cuts but managed to tuck hers away inside her hollow leg along with half a large baked potato.

We were at the table eating when Betty said, "Please pass the salt, *Angela*."

Mr. Gandy laid his silver down. Betty made a great show of studying the cap on the crystal saltshaker. I was beginning to understand her way of operating.

I followed Mr. Gandy into the kitchen.

"I feel silly," Mr. Gandy said. "You've had us calling you Roberta all afternoon."

"She must have heard Ray use my name."

He poured himself a scotch and me a ginger ale. As long as I had him alone, I asked him what Headquarters had to say about Betty. He had slipped away for a half hour during the melon-eating, so I assumed he'd been on the phone.

"I'll let you know when there's news," he said. He plunked a straw into my ginger ale, which made me feel eight years old.

After dinner we moved to the living room. The woodwork glowed as though it had been rubbed that very day, and a long muzzle-loader over the fireplace caught Betty's eye. The poodle crossed the room and laid his head on Mr. Gandy's leg.

"Hello, Estevan," Mr. Gandy said. He rubbed the dog behind its ears until it dropped into a heap.

On the wall there was an old painting of three round-headed children with bows around their necks. "The one with curls is my great-grand-mother," Mrs. Gandy said. The artist had work in the National Gallery, she mentioned.

With their great serious eyes and straight mouths the children looked as though they had come back from the dead, though maybe not all the way.

"That portrait is a piece of American history," Mr. Gandy said.

I guess Mrs. Gandy knew this to be the windup to a story, because she asked Mr. Gandy not to tell it. "Our guests don't want to hear that awful business," she said.

He wouldn't be stopped. The scotch he gripped was his third or fourth, and his face was pink and his voice bright like brass as he told how the children's parents had been murdered by Indians. "Slaughtered—throats cut! And the children tied in place to see them bleed out. Imagine their lives, having seen such a thing! But no—you can't imagine a thing like that. It would make you into something altogether different."

He rested the glass on a shelf made by his stomach and smiled at the poodle, who was watching him. "I see you, old friend," he said, and he stretched to touch the dog's head again while Mrs. Gandy from her chair two yards away burned holes in the side of his face. At last he felt the temperature.

"Did I say something wrong? They've all been dead for many de-cades," he said.

Mrs. Gandy didn't speak, only glared.

"What is it?" Mr. Gandy said. Then he looked at me, and dismay cov-ered his face. "Excuse me," he said. "I'm awfully stupid."

Mrs. Gandy said, "My God, Alex." She got out of her chair and left the room.

42

Their embarrassment was interesting to me. They view me as something fragile, I decided. Something damaged.

"This portrait must have been made before the parents were *keyhole*," Betty said. "Most people will not pay to make a portrait of some orphan brother and sister."

Mr. Gandy was so visibly rattled that his poodle had stood up. "Now, now, Estevan," Mr. Gandy said. "Sit. Let's change the subject, ladies."

"You have a big house," Betty said. "What is your job?"

"I'm retired from the florin service," he said.

"Don't know what that is," Betty said.

"I meant to say *foreign* service."

"Still don't know. You have work with this girl's father?"

"What's on TV?" I said.

"Yes," Mr. Gandy said. "Her father and I are old colleagues."

"I am surprise he will let her drive that Scamp. She is too small. I don't see anybody else who is so small drive a car and go around by herself. I am worry about her maybe. She have said she will help me, but I think, How? She is not an adult."

"If it were not for me and that Scamp," I said, "you would have got your hand chopped off."

"I haven't heard that part yet," Mr. Gandy said.

"I'm just talking about a very angry old woman with a knife as big as your shoe," I said.

"I think maybe this girl's father has run away," Betty said.

"Mr. Gandy knows where my father is!"

"Who is Mr. Gandy?" Betty said.

"I mean Mr. Howell!" I said.

"What will you do, Mr. Howell?" Betty said to Mr. Gandy.

"I don't know what I will do," he said. "I'm lost."

"Nobody know what they will do!" Betty said. "I never have stroke a dog before."

Mr. Gandy jumped on the new topic. "My goodness, would you like to stroke Estevan?"

Betty frowned. She got up off the flowered chintz chair she'd been sitting on and bent to rub her hand along the back of Estevan's neck.

"*Curly,*" she said. She smelled her hand, looked at me, and went on stroking.

"He's just an old pet-grade boy," Mr. Gandy said. "Did you know that gray is not an authorized color for a poodle? And yet here he is, a poodle and gray! Aren't you, old boy? What do you think of Betty? Is she nice?"

"What do you think of Chinese person touch you?" Betty said to the dog.

43

"I am so sleepy," Betty said.

I intended to have a word alone with her, but it had to wait while Mrs. Gandy showed us to bed one at a time. Betty was first, then me. In the bedroom Mrs. Gandy stripped the mattress and put new sheets on, though the old ones appeared clean. She had me sit down with her while she ran a smoothing hand over the chenille bedspread. "Tell me how you and Betty came together," she said.

I told her the same story I'd given Mr. Gandy, all vagueness and holes.

"I don't believe that, Angela."

"Betty may well be lying," I said. "We'll have to let the analysts sort it out."

"You know that's not what I mean," she said quietly.

Well, yes. I did know. But this was my story, and I couldn't change it now. This pushing back against an obvious cover was a very frustrating quality of Mrs. Gandy's. Her husband had not believed my story, either, I'm sure, but he'd had the courtesy to accept it.

She asked me whether I had something to sleep in, and I told her no. "There is probably something of Julie's here," she said. She brought some folded pajamas from a drawer. Then she started up the questions again.

MRS. GANDY: Where is Ray, Angela?
ME: I told you he's on his honeymoon.
MRS. GANDY: You said he was engaged. Has he been drinking awfully much?
ME: Less, lately, if you want to know.

I'm not sure why I let this bit of truth out. She knew his history, and even though I didn't want to talk about him, I wanted her opinion.

MRS. GANDY: Is he in a program?

ME: No, he's not in a program. He just decided to dry out.

MRS. GANDY: It was so difficult for him before, you remember.

ME: Well, yes.

MRS. GANDY: We've all been worried about both of you. How is he doing?

ME: I don't know. I've been helping him some.

MRS. GANDY: Helping him how?

ME: Just bringing him tangerines, and sitting with him. Listening to him talk.

MRS. GANDY: What does he talk about?

ME: Oh, chickens. Africa. Someone named Celeste.

MRS. GANDY: You know who Celeste is, dear.

ME: No, I don't.

She studied me a long time.

MRS. GANDY: What was your mother's name?

ME: Why do you ask me that?

MRS. GANDY: Well, I'm a mother, and I'd like to think that if I were gone, my daughters would remember my name.

ME: I do remember my mother's name.

MRS. GANDY: What was it?

ME: There's no need to delve into all of this. Let me get those pajamas on.

MRS. GANDY: Angela. Celeste was Ray's wife.

ME: Oh.

MRS. GANDY: I'm starting to see what's happened. Did you even know that Ray had been married?

ME: No.

MRS. GANDY: Well. I never met her. They married in Stanleyville, and we never saw Ray then. The only contact was by radio.

Alex was posted at the embassy in Leopoldville, and we were there, too, the girls and I. You remember that.

ME: Yes.

MRS. GANDY: Ray was quite alone in Stanleyville. No one at the consulate up there knew who he was. I mean, they all *knew* him, but they knew him as a businessman, not as an Agency officer. He had some elaborate cover operation going— something to do with a cigarette factory, or a beer concern. He'd spent years building it. And he was quite on his own. You can't blame him for wanting a friend. You expect people to have friends. Marrying her was more complicated, because she wasn't American. The Agency doesn't encourage that. But there was a child.

ME: A daughter?

MRS. GANDY: Yes. And Ray wanted her to become a U.S. citizen, so he married Celeste, and Alex smoothed it out somehow with Headquarters and got the girl a passport.

ME: Okay.

MRS. GANDY: She was younger than you. I never saw her. She would have been four, I think, when the Simba rebellion happened.

ME: What happened to her?

MRS. GANDY: Well, we heard that she and Celeste had both been killed. The news was very broken—the consular staff in Stanleyville had been taken hostage, and the Simbas controlled the airport, so we really didn't know what was happening, outside of what Ray said in his messages to Alex. Then those stopped, too, and we didn't know whether Ray was dead or alive. A long time passed with no word. And then the Belgian paratroopers landed, and there was a horrible massacre, but some got out, and Ray was among them. And when he showed up in Leopoldville, he had you with him, and he said you were Angela. We heard she was killed, we said. And he said no—if we'd heard that, then there had been a miscommunication. Angela wasn't dead, she was here.

ME: Please don't talk about this with anyone, Mrs. Gandy.

MRS. GANDY: But who are you, then?

ME: There is just no need to delve into all of this. Let's not do it.

MRS. GANDY: I've always known something was wrong. You were older than you should have been, by years. Alex said not to talk about it. You were traumatized and wouldn't let go of Ray, but I figured—

ME: Enough. I don't want to talk about this anymore.

MRS. GANDY: We'll talk tomorrow.

ME: No. We'll never talk about it. There is nothing to be gained from talking about it.

MRS. GANDY: I'm not sure that's true.

ME: I appreciate all of your kindness to me. There's something you don't understand. When you live a cover, you can't be picking through it all the time. You just live it.

I could tell that what I said did not satisfy her. She left that topic, but there were other things she wanted to know.

MRS. GANDY: Do you have any friends?

ME: Of course I do.

MRS. GANDY: Tell me about some of them.

ME: There are so many.

MRS. GANDY: Who is your best friend?

ME: It would be Helen Sanchez.

MRS. GANDY: What sorts of things do you and Helen talk about?

ME: Typical girl things. Boys and so forth. Please can I go to bed now?

MRS. GANDY: Yes. Do you know that you are always welcome here?

ME: Thank you. I'll be fine once we figure out where to put Betty. I want that project out of my hands.

MRS. GANDY: We'll ride Babe and Red again tomorrow.

ME: Okay.
MRS. GANDY: Will you be all right alone in here?
ME: Why not? I'm fine alone.

She said good night and left, and I was just as fine as I said I would be.

44

Later, when the house was quiet, I crept along the hall. I found Betty sitting cross-legged on a high, twin-sized antique bed, bathed and dressed in checked pajamas, combing her wet hair with her fingers in a claw shape.

"What are you say to that man about me?" Betty asked.

"Never mind that. You broke your word."

"Huh?"

"The deal was that you'd say nothing about my father!"

"I have not made that deal."

"In the future I'll know not to trust you."

She carried on with the finger-combing. "Why have you lie to him about your father?"

"I don't know what you're talking about."

"You tell him your father has gone away to be marry. I don't think that is true."

"Can everybody just leave my father out of it?"

"Because if *that* is true, you will also have tell me that same thing! We have been ride in Scamp all those hours, so long. Why not tell me if your father has gone away to be marry? It is *not* true."

"I don't like you," I said.

"Mr. Howell can get me a passport?"

"He could help you, if you'd give him a reason."

"Mm. People will usually want something back for help you."

"That's business."

"Chinese think business is for capitalist making money."

"Oh, please. Now I'm going to throw up."

"I have not serve Chinese revolution very well, but I will never betray my people's revolution."

"What are you talking about?"

"Try to understand what I will say to you, girl. You want me to do something I will never, never do."

I was surprised by a flutter of respect for that little brown space alien. I put it away. "You're nuts," I said.

She unfolded her legs and stepped out of the borrowed pajamas. My patchwork print dress went on over her head.

"What are you doing?" I said.

"Leaving."

"No, we are staying tonight."

"I am leaving tonight."

"We're in the middle of the woods," I said.

"I can walk out of the woods," Betty said. "Can walk one thousand mile."

She knelt to buckle her cloth and rubber shoes.

"You've got no way to live," I said.

"It is easy to live. Nobody starve in U.S."

The hallway was dark except for a soft yellow line at the foot of the Gandys' bedroom door. The Chinese moved quickly, as though she had planned her way. I touched something and it clattered against the floor. Estevan barked.

I ran after Betty. Lights came on behind us.

Outside, there was no moon. The air was wet and sharp. In the distance, a chorus of hepped-up voices answered Estevan's barking. Coyotes.

I felt Betty's hand on my arm. We ran over the soft, crunching gravel.

I had chased Betty to drag her back, and now I was getting into the Scamp with her. I don't know why my mind changed. I stomped on the gas pedal. The porch light came on. The engine heaved but wouldn't catch. Estevan lurched out the door, followed by Mrs. Gandy in a belted white caftan.

My throttle-stomping had flooded the carburetor. But the hour's wait in front of Sears and Roebuck, which had seemed such an inconvenience at the time, now served me well, as I had used that time to study the Scamp owner's manual from the glove compartment. I held the gas pedal to the floor and turned the key again, and this time the engine coughed twice and roared awake. The clean gravel churned and flew.

Mrs. Gandy watched us go, straight in her white robe, holding Estevan by his collar.

45

Sometimes it is better not to think the big thoughts. You want to focus on *what's in front of you*. And yet the inside of a car at night seems like it was made for brooding, and there are places in West Virginia where, because of the mountains, you can't get anything on the radio but static and weird electric whines. Weird popping strings and deep elastic hums. The world is dark like a box you're inside of. Maybe you can sit through an hour of it without thinking, but to not think for a second hour is difficult with only the snapping electric sounds and nothing else to distract you from whatever's in your head.

I kept seeing those three awful children with the bows around their necks. I imagined the bows coming loose and the heads dropping off those rigid bodies in their starched old-fashioned outfits. Doll heads rolling in grass. The night mind is different from the daytime mind.

My fists held the hard plastic wheel, and I thought of Ray's big-knuckled fists pulling the wet sheet tightly around him during the time when he was sickest and didn't understand where he was. So he'd had a real daughter. I could have guessed it, and maybe I'd known. That passport. I had studied it many times, wondering. The picture hardly mattered—babies look so much alike, and seldom resemble the people they grow up to be. That the year of birth was so far off had never been a problem. It was like Betty said—people don't look and are easy to fool.

There were numerous reasons for Ray and me never to have talked about that real daughter. I understood. It is a principle in clandestine work that you only tell a person what she needs to know in order to do her part, and there was no need—no operational need—for me to know about Ray's wife and child. The thing that did upset me rather badly was the thought of what it had cost Ray to keep it all to himself. Perhaps it had cost him heavily. I thought about all those nights when

I'd been upstairs with my shortwave listening to those goofy English lessons, while Ray was downstairs cracking the ice tray against the countertop and emptying glasses of bourbon into his body. A person never knows what's in another person's mind. I wondered whether Ray had not allowed himself to suffer too much. He could have told me about that daughter safely, because I am better at keeping a secret than almost anyone. To keep it by himself was too hard! I could hardly bear to think about it now. I choked back my sniveling so as not to wake Betty.

Red and blue lights flashed behind me, and I jumped. Colored shadows crawled over the dashboard. I pulled the Scamp over to the soft edge of the road. All right: so this was it. But the police car only swerved and went by, its siren like a spade on my chest. Betty had sat up in the back seat. She lay down again.

I felt completely lost. And then, all at once, I knew what I had to do. Ray wouldn't like it, but I intended to bring this up with him. I would tell him that I knew about this daughter. That's all. And if he wanted to tell me about her—well, I doubted he would. But at least she would have been spoken of, and her existence revived in this way.

I felt a little lighter inside. Ray was my friend, and I was his. The hours to go before daylight didn't seem so long anymore. From time to time I saw a pair of eyes like dimes looking into my headlights from close to the ground—small creatures at their business of breaking acorns. Ray and I were that way, too: busy animals put on earth to crack things open and eat what was inside them.

I was sleepy and let my outside tires go off the road. Betty shouted. It did me some good. There was no point in killing us both in a car wreck out here in the mountains.

Some color came into the sky. My eyes felt filmed over, and I can't say how badly I desired to brush my teeth. Betty climbed up front.

"Where are we?" she said.

"Kentucky. We're going out West for a while."

"Sign says we are going out South."

I explained to her that even on a trip out West, one is bound to go north or south from time to time, because of the nature of roads. "Also, signs can be wrong."

Folded on the seat was an Esso map of Kentucky. I switched on the interior light and told Betty the number of the expressway to look for. Betty was surprised to learn that the Scamp had a light that could be turned on inside. She studied the map without comment, then folded it wrong.

I pulled over to study it myself. I had expected us to be on the expressway by now. For hours we'd threaded through the terrain as a creek would do. But my head was murky, and I couldn't make out where we were.

Later, when we did come to the expressway, we found that it was under construction. In the early weak daylight we saw clean notches cut through the mountain and two rows of concrete pilings, partly spanned. Sheets of plastic hung ragged at the raw end of a bridge deck. Steel bars jutted from it like fish bones.

46

By daylight I was a severe kind of tired. A white barn with red mud around it floated near the road. Some starlings had lined up on the silver roof, and their feet were stuck in the new paint, I imagined. I was consulting the Kentucky map while cresting a hill and holding the steering wheel with my left knee when Betty said, "Uh-oh. Cow in road!"

I stood on the brake, and the Scamp slid sideways. One wheel dropped off the pavement. We rocked once and were still.

The cow was black. It pulled its big head out of the ditch grass and rolled an eye.

"You should not look at the map when you drive!" Betty said.

"This free map was no bargain!" I said. "We're not even on it! This so-called '*Happy Motoring* Guide.'" I wadded it up.

"If a car will come over the hill behind us now, we are going to die," Betty said.

I tried to reverse the Scamp uphill, but the tire that had come off the road only spun. In front of us, the cow blocked the way. When I honked at her, she showed me her square hindquarters.

"No more setting out without a plan!" I said.

Evidently this cow had been honked at before. My honking didn't alarm her in any way. She had never had shrill Communist slogans shouted at her by an arm-waving Chinese, however. That was new. Away she jogged, with Betty jogging after her. Betty looked different, chasing a cow down the road. Sitting in the car with her for hour upon hour it was easy to forget how small she was.

I put the Scamp in drive and touched the gas, nudging it down-hill and back onto the road. Around the bend, I caught Betty waving goodbye to the cow. The cow had gone back into her pasture at a spot where the fence was down.

My stomach felt as though it had some air in it. The lesson I was learning, not for the first time, was that you can go without food and you can go without sleep, but you can't go without food *and* without sleep. Betty, having napped and been for a jog, now bounced on the front seat and sang a Red Chinese grade school song, which she translated as she went. "All the flowers love him, baby goats also love him, people in field love him," etc. She did not explain who *him* was. The song had hand movements to go with it. Politely I asked her to be quiet and stop bouncing or else I would certainly lose my mind, and she crossed her arms and went into one of her funks.

47

We passed a sign saying KNOXVILLE CITY LIMITS. I could not find it on our Kentucky map. Yet the town was of some size, judging by the vastness of its GM dealership. We stopped at a café called Roby's, I believe, and Betty cursed me for a long time in Chinese while we waited for some menus. I startled her by cursing back in imitation Chinese.

"Don't this one speak English?" the waitress said.

"Count your blessings."

"Where's she from?"

"Formosa," I said. It just came out.

"Tell her I said, *Hello and welcome to Tennessee.*"

"Excuse me, what?"

"*Hello and welcome to Tennessee.*"

I studied the waitress, confused. She appeared to be wearing white eye shadow. You only saw it when she turned a certain way.

"Go on, tell her," the waitress said. "I know you speak her language. I heard you talking when I come over here."

Feeling that it would be the simplest way, I spoke some more of my imitation Chinese.

Betty sat up straight. Syllables came out of her mouth.

"She don't sound happy!"

"Their language always sounds grumpy like that," I said. "She asks me to thank you and to tell you she would like to try your American-style bacon and two fried eggs. I'll have the biscuits and gravy, please."

Later the waitress brought the cook out to see us, I mean only to look. He stood in the kitchen doorway.

So this was Tennessee.

As we were eating, a girl in a brown leotard and bell-bottom jeans came to speak with the cook. "I have to give you back that money for the orphans in Palookadong," she said.

I eavesdropped. Some boys at college had signed her up for a coin drive to buy record players for the blind orphans at Palookadong, so the orphans could listen to *Time* magazine. The girl collected almost twenty dollars in an oatmeal canister. Then she found out that Palookadong was not a real place. She asked the cook to remember how much money he had contributed.

"A dollar."

"He never give you any dollar," the waitress with the white eyelids said. "Look in that can and see have you got a dirty nickel that was run over by a train. He might've give you that."

"No," the cook said, "I give her several quarters to help those blond orphans."

"They was blind, you idiot."

"It was raining that day," the cook said. "I remember you come in here with your hair dripping. Isn't that right?"

The girl's hair was long, straight, and reddish gold in color. "Maybe it was raining," she said.

"Either that or you had washed it," he said. "But it was sure dripping!" He jabbed his finger at a pin on her leotard. "Why would you waste a vote on McGovern?"

"George speaks to my generation," the girl said. "Bobby Kennedy called George the most decent man in the Senate."

"That's like calling him a clean turd."

"Those two over there speak Formosan," the waitress mentioned.

The girl in the brown leotard eyed us shyly and smiled at Betty. I worried she might come over, but then the cook announced that he did not want his quarters back, and to my relief the girl skipped out the door.

It was my first time eating biscuits with sausage gravy. They made an excellent inexpensive breakfast. Betty ate her eggs with a spoon.

48

Betty asked me whether gum-chewing would be healthy for her teeth. It couldn't have hurt them any. I encouraged her to give it a second try. I showed her how to put a penny in the Lions Club gum machine and slide the lever to get a gumball out. On the way out of Roby's we got her several gumballs. Then, in the parking lot, the right rear tire of the Scamp was flat.

With the biscuits and sausage gravy in me, I took it in my stride. "This is why we carry a spare," I said.

I was at the trunk when someone spoke behind me. It was the girl in the brown leotard, accompanied by a long, slouching fellow with a fringe of mustache and bangs in his eyes.

"They told us your friend is from Formosa," she said.

"That's right."

"Eeyore can help you change your tire."

The boy lifted the spare out and dropped it. It rolled away. Off he went after it, Roman sandals slapping the pavement. His pants had colored stripes down the length of them, and the sandals looked as though they had not come off his feet for several weeks.

As he rolled the tire back across the parking lot he appeared sad and embarrassed. Even the feet with their long, groping toes expressed melancholy. The girl, however, was just as bright and cheery as you could ever want. I had the jack in my hands, and she said, "Eeyore, you can do that." Eeyore puzzled over how to fit the handle on.

"I never met anyone from Formosa before," the girl said.

Betty stayed in the Scamp during all this, working on her gum-balls. She added them to her mouth one by one, with long, attentive intervals between. In an effort to dominate the situation, I led the girl to Betty's window and said, "This is my friend who is visiting from Formosa and does not speak a word of English."

"What is her name?" the girl said.

"Ding Lo."

"Hello, Ding. My name is Renee." Renee shook Betty's hand through the window then asked me my name. I told her something which I immediately forgot.

The boy dropped the jack handle on his sandaled foot and began to softly moan. Renee hustled over, cooing. There was a lengthy fuss during which I tried to remember what I had said my name was. Renee had Eeyore limp over to some grass and sit. He had sustained a short laceration on his pointer toe.

I levered up the jack in the spot where Eeyore had placed it. Next I was interrupted by a woman with a scarf around her neck whistling at me from a white Chevy Caprice.

The woman left her car. She studied the jack for only a moment, then took the handle away from me and used it to knock the jack out from under the Scamp. Where Eeyore had placed it, she said, it would only have crumpled the sheet metal. "You need to get your friend out of the car as well," she added.

I pulled Betty out. The woman raised the jack under the rear bumper. "Look how I'm doing this," she said. "You want to loosen the lug nuts before you get the tire all the way off the ground." In her blouse, scarf, tailored skirt, and tall zipper boots she applied herself to the task while the injured hippie boy lay vaporing, attended by his cheerful Renee. Inside of ten minutes my Good Samaritan had the spare on and had showed me the bright head of a nail in the tread of my tire. "Have that patched at your first opportunity," she said. "Not plugged, but patched." She had on large, green-framed sunglasses. She frowned at her wristwatch and left.

Eeyore was back on his feet now. He asked to be introduced to Ding.

Betty said something in Chinese. The hippie couple turned to me, waiting to hear my translation.

"She said she is surprised at how outgoing the Tennesseans are. We have met so many new friends today."

Eeyore followed up with a series of questions. Why America? Did you come on a boat? What's for breakfast in Formosa? Are there freaks there like Renee and me? Do they have a gassy youth scene? Betty gave long answers which I pretended to translate. Then Renee did some cartwheels.

I put Betty back in the Scamp. Eeyore asked if we could give them a ride to campus. After establishing which way campus was, I told him we definitely couldn't. "We have to keep moving the other way," I said.

"Where are you headed?"

"Nashville!"

He appeared confused. "Nashville's *this* way," he said. Renee had him give us his mother's phone number. "We don't have a phone where we dwell," she explained. There was another fuss as Eeyore searched his pants pockets for a scrap of paper. None could be found. The pockets were nearly empty, he explained, because the pants had just been washed.

Finally he wrote out the number longways on a cigarette, which Betty smoked as soon as we were moving again.

"Let's get the hell out of Tennessee," I said.

49

Nothing is simple, however. The man at Sears and Roebuck would not patch the nail hole because there was also an abrasion on the sidewall. "Truthfully, you need a whole set," he said.

That couldn't be right, I told him, because I'd had a new set put on mere days ago.

He took me around to look at the Armando Snacki tires. None of them matched, and the front right tire had fibers showing through the rubber. The new set would cost me one hundred forty-five dollars, and it would be an hour before he could put them on the Scamp because he had to replace the parking brake cable on a Ford pickup first.

Inside Sears I followed an interested Betty down aisles of house paint and waited while she stared at a long bin of record albums. We stood at a wall of televisions. The soap opera faces were a little pinker on one screen, a little greener on the next. When we came to the women's clothing Betty's mouth clicked open, and I saw her eyes go soft and vague. She stopped at a rack of dresses and stood there like a child in the cereal aisle.

"Nobody cares if you touch them," I said.

She scraped one coat hanger along the chrome.

There was a pitiful tenderness in the little Maoist's gaze. At the shoe department, she lost all resemblance to her former self. She resembled a spilled Pepsi. I reminded her, "You have a hundred bucks tucked away somewhere on your body. Buy whatever you want."

Betty put her finger on one shoe, then another. Then the lady measured her foot. Betty smiled bashfully when her ankle was touched. The first pair of shoes she tried on was a set of espadrilles with a very tall cork heel, and she fell over into a chair when she tried to walk on them. It was the first time I saw her laugh, and downright strange.

After ninety minutes of the dresses, shoes, sun hats, and shoulder bags I was both bored and starving. A big breakfast will always make you hungry for a big lunch. We found a coffee shop in the mall and ordered some chili dogs. Betty speared the wiener on a fork and took small bites off it, ignoring the bun. Her new dress was pink gingham with a white spread collar.

"You are quite the clothes hound," I said. "I didn't think you Communists went in for a lot of clothes-shopping."

"Everybody like to have some new things," she said. "Maybe now I will blend."

"You will never blend while eating your chili dog with a fork," I said. "Look here. See how I do it?" I picked my dog up in the bun and bit the end off.

"Messy way."

"That's what this is for." I fluttered a paper napkin.

On ways of eating, Betty wouldn't be steered. She took lots of very small bites and bent low over the plate, though I told her that looks coarse to the Western eye. "You eat like a pet from the dish," I said.

"You eat like a squirrel," she said. She straightened her spine against the chair back and twitched her head as though she were monitoring the whole room while chewing.

Earlier, while Betty was waiting to check out at Sears, I had left her and bought two hairbrushes, a light blue one and a green one. I presented the green one to her now. She was so surprised and pleased with it, it made me feel a little poor. They were cheap plastic hairbrushes, and the only reason I had bought two was so I wouldn't have to share the blue one.

50

Back in the Scamp, Betty got to work thrashing at her hair with the new brush. She used her whole arm very fast and vigorously, as though she meant not only to brush the hair but to teach it an important lesson. Then she made two long braids and tied each one with a piece of green yarn. I don't know where she got the yarn. When she was done with that she slid her new white tennis shoes off, folded her legs on the seat, and began to sing in English in a queer, quiet falsetto: "*Why, somebody? Why will people break up?*"

Soon she went to sleep in her easy way.

We got onto the new expressway, which was straight and monotonous. The sky was dull like smoked foil, the pavement flawlessly smooth. My eyes were sore.

My head became empty, and then I saw a fat old woman in a housedress run into the road with a platter of food. I swerved. Betty threw her arms out.

"Sleeping! Wake up!"

It was true. I was very tired, but I wanted to keep going until we made Virginia.

But first, the new expressway ran out. I got onto an old stop-and-start U.S. highway. I left Betty dozing in the Scamp while I stepped into a truck stop. At the counter a man in a denim shirt was tearing packets of sugar three at a time for his coffee. A shred of paper fell in. His hand trembled when he used the spoon to dip it out.

I asked him where I could get on the expressway again.

"Past Bristol," he said. "I'm not headed that way." He wanted to know where my parents were.

Too tired to make something up, I simply told him, "It's all right," and got my coffee and left.

We had exited the parking lot when Betty said she needed to use the bathroom. I asked her why she had not done that before we left, and she barked at me in Chinese.

I turned the Scamp around and told her not to speak to anyone.

While I waited in the Scamp, something changed in the look of the day. Shadows came out where there had not been any before, and a gray bush beside a gas meter was now a green holly plant. I got out to wake myself up and look at the sky. The haze had clotted, organizing itself into clouds. A lot of small birds were moving around.

A woman was looking at me from a phone booth across the lot. Her brown hair was draped in barrettes on both sides of her head. When our eyes met she turned her back to me like a figure on a cuckoo clock, smooth and mechanical.

I thought I must be hallucinating again, because I knew that woman's boots. I had seen them before, and her scarf as well, and that didn't seem possible. But I wasn't hallucinating. There by the phone booth was her white Chevy Caprice.

51

I got into the Scamp to drive away, but something stopped me. If she was the person GRISTLE had sent to shoot me on the sidewalk, why had she changed my tire?

I blocked her car with the Scamp. I walked right up to the phone booth and straight-armed the door. "Tell me who you are," I said.

"Back up and let me come out."

"Are you with the FBI? If so, you are required by law to tell me."

She laughed at me. "How old are you, kid?"

"Nineteen."

"I'm twenty-nine. Now we're both liars."

I let her get out of the booth and she gave me an odd, sultry "Thank you." I noticed her unusual eyes. The blue irises had dark rings around them. It puzzled me that I hadn't noticed them before, until I remembered the sunglasses. She asked me why I was following her.

"Don't be cute," I said. "*You're* following *me*."

"It's been a while since anyone called me cute," she said.

A dozen thoughts fell through my head. I couldn't read her face—there was too much going on there. The mouth had a smirk on it, but strawberry blotches had come out in front of both ears. She looked past me, then down at my hands. Her hand went slowly to her pocket.

I shoved her and ran. I had left the Scamp idling. She was smart, though. Instead of chasing me, she simply got into the Scamp on the passenger side. It was the same trick Betty had used.

"Are you going to shoot me?" I said.

"Shoot you? Why would I shoot you?"

"Get out or I will crash the car."

"Easy, now," she said. "Let's talk. Let's figure this out."

"What do you want from me?"

"Well, I was following you. I wanted you not to see me."

"Who told you to follow me?"

"I'm working with Ray," she said. "I'm on Ray's side."

Across the lot, Betty was standing on the curb with her chin in the air, looking for the Scamp. I felt as though I were watching her in a silent movie. She spotted me, and I saw her come a few steps. Then she saw that I wasn't alone, and she stopped.

I reversed the Scamp in an arc, backing onto a curb.

"Why don't you let me drive?" the woman said.

I didn't answer. I just drove, leaving Betty behind in the parking lot.

"All right. We'll do this if you want."

The look of everything changed again. Shadows blurred, and it rained. I was stuck and felt childish, persisting in harmful behavior, but I didn't know what else to do. This was not the way in which Ray had promised to contact me.

The woman smelled like cigarettes and shampoo. She had to remind me where the switch was for the windshield wipers. She asked me where I was taking her.

"Is Ray sick?" I said.

I could see that she was considering.

"Don't consider, just tell me! How is he?"

"Ray's all right. He's worried about you."

There was a fidget in my steering, the kind of thing that scared Betty awake.

"You cannot keep driving without sleep," the woman said. "I've seen you drifting all over the road. You'll kill someone. Look at you, Angela. You're so tired, you look like a little old man."

"Shut up about that," I said. And yet something broke. I had to pull over.

"Go on and cry," she said. "Nobody minds it." She lit a cigarette and waited for me to get straight and clean up my face on my sleeve.

52

ME: Tell me who you are.

WOMAN: I'm with the Agency. We met once at the Farm, but you don't seem to remember.

ME: No, I don't.

WOMAN: I caught you hiding in the library.

ME: Oh. That was you?

WOMAN: My hair was different then.

ME: I wasn't hiding, I was reading. What is your name?

WOMAN: Marilyn.

ME: Ray told me to stay clear of Agency people.

WOMAN: I was keeping an eye on you, that's all.

ME: How long have you been following me?

WOMAN: Only today. We found you by luck.

ME: How?

WOMAN: I can't tell you everything!

ME: When have you spoken to Ray?

WOMAN: I'm sorry. I'm supposed to be tailing you, not briefing you. I suspect we've both been waiting on instructions. Isn't that right?

ME: I don't think you've talked to Ray at all.

WOMAN: I've spoken to someone who has spoken to Ray. No more on that, okay? Tell me about Ding.

ME: Ding is just some crazy Oriental girl I picked up. She's harmless.

WOMAN: What does she know about you?

ME: I told her a cover story. Anyway, I've got her number. She's vulnerable.

WOMAN: How's that?

ME: Her immigration is not in order.

WOMAN: You shouldn't be traveling with someone like that. You're not thinking.

ME: Of course I'm thinking! Things come up and I deal with them. You must have put a transmitter on my car when you changed the tire. Is that what you did?

WOMAN: You're funny.

ME: What happens now?

WOMAN: Now I get to call my boss and tell him I've been made by a fourteen-year-old girl. That'll be pleasant. I'll do it tomorrow.

ME: Tomorrow, not tonight?

WOMAN: You're not the Cuban Missile Crisis. It'll keep.

ME: You ought to have changed vehicles after you helped me with the tire. That's how I made you, by that white Chevy.

WOMAN: Why don't you take me back to that white Chevy now, okay? There happens to be a few thousand dollars' worth of taxpayer-owned equipment in the trunk.

ME: And the keys are in the ignition.

WOMAN: And the keys. Right.

53

The Chevy was there, but Betty was gone. I couldn't believe it. After all my work managing and looking after her, I had let her go in this stupid way. It made me furious that she couldn't have waited forty-five minutes. A waitress told us she'd left with a notoriously friendly truck driver named Skeet.

The rain stopped after dark. In case Betty was looking for me, I stood outside the truck stop under a white fluorescent bulb with beetles pinging off of it. A big, meaty moth kept knocking, too. The wet blacktop was streaked with yellow light from the truck stop sign. I don't remember the name of the place.

I ate a plate dinner of sliced ham with canned corn and pinto beans. I sat at the window, watching. Marilyn wolfed down a salad, and then we took the two cars half a mile up U.S. 11 to the Crown Motor Court. The cover of the phone book said Kingsport, Tennessee.

Marilyn moved around the room, adjusting lights and the fan by the window. "I've seen worse," she said of the room. I had, too, and recently. She saw me eyeing her big suitcase and flashed a smile.

She brought out a bottle of gin and poured herself a healthy shot in a paper cup.

I asked her, "Is this something all you people do?"

She twisted the cap down on the bottle using the side of her wrist, and I saw a whiff of anxiety rise off her.

"Never mind," she said.

She fumbled to unzip her boots. The leather creaked when she slid them off. She settled on top of the bedspread, knees up, back against the headboard. She pointed. "Pitch me a pack of cigarettes and my lighter, would you?"

Her purse was quite full of objects, including pens, peppermints, blank index cards, an orange, and a box of raisins. The leather cigarette case had a long brown hair hanging off of it. I pitched the case to her, hair and all. She pulled smoke from her cigarette as though she were climbing a rope.

I noticed a roaring in my ears. I sat on a chair.

I asked her how much trouble she would be in because I had made her. She rolled her head, stretching her neck. "It depends how things turn out. The career's in a funny place, you know."

"No, I don't know."

"Well, I'm assigned to follow the daughter of an American citizen inside the U.S. This is not considered a plum assignment. Ordinarily it *would* be a Bureau matter."

"Why isn't it?"

"It soon will be, if I keep screwing up."

"How long have you been with the Agency?" I asked.

"Couple years."

"Have you been overseas yet?"

"Sure. Can't gab about it. They mostly kept me buried at my embassy job."

"Run any agents?"

"A couple that I inherited."

"Didn't you ever recruit one?"

No answer. She only looked at me.

"How do the men treat you?" I said.

"Mostly not so good. That's between you and me, please."

"What, do they have you bring coffee?"

"I don't mind bringing coffee. That's not what I'm talking about."

There was a TV set on the dresser. Someone had written *Maggie* with a fingertip in the dust on the picture tube.

"I got called back early," Marilyn said.

"What happened?"

"I lost an asset." She rubbed the heel of a palm against her forehead.

"What do you mean, lost?"

"Lost, lost. Not coming back." She blinked and made her eyes gape. "I made a technical error. I had to move a person across a border. A simple job—that's why they gave it to me. She had a legitimate passport. I was merely serving as travel agent.

"I sent her to the consulate to have her passport stamped. She'd get the visa just before lunch, get straight on the train, and take the evening ferry. No standing around. I even visited the consulate first. It was closed weekends, so I put her there on a Monday. It was the Monday after Easter."

She gave me a bleak look.

"And?"

"In this particular country," Marilyn said, "they have these screwy things called 'bank holidays.' I didn't know—I'd been there three weeks. These banks holidays, they pop up when you aren't looking for them. Monday night—the Monday after Easter—we get a call from my colleague in Calais, the one who was supposed to meet the person coming off the boat. The person hasn't showed. 'Well, did she ever get on the boat?' my C.O.S. wants to know. 'I didn't follow her onto the boat,' I said. 'Was I supposed to?'

"The C.O.S. asked if her papers were in order. I told him about sending her to the consulate, and he jumped up out of his chair."

"Couldn't you have arranged the visa yourself?" I said.

"Sure I could have," Marilyn said. "I knew how to do that from spy college. But I didn't see the need, because I didn't know the consulate would be closed on the Monday after Easter. I'm not one of these foreign service brats who spent all her summers abroad. My father was a D.C. police officer."

"What happened then?"

"Well, we tried to find her. I found out she'd been calling my apartment all afternoon. Then she'd called her uncle in Aix-en-Provence. Later we learned the other side had her."

"Was she an important asset?"

"No. Her uncle was, and she was important to him. That's where she was going—to join his family. She had no idea what he was into, or who I was."

"That's when you got sent home?"

"Right. Only it doesn't sound so bad when you say it that way, 'sent home.' There's more to it—a lot of talking and waiting on cables. Then more talking. Here's the thing with the Agency: yes, everything's sneaky and secret, but it's also a government job."

I asked her what had made her take up with the Agency to begin with.

"I don't know. The standard line is that there are two reasons why a woman goes into clandestine work. One is that she lost someone, like a father, husband, brother, or son, and she's grieving and seeks revenge. You know about this? They teach us this stuff."

"I never heard it before."

"And the other reason is a pathology which prevents her from enjoying a normal domestic life."

"Does either one describe you?"

"They both describe me, but that doesn't mean the principle is correct." She refilled her cup.

I asked her whether she had considered a different line of work.

"I have thought about becoming a park ranger," she said. She went to the sink.

I wanted to sleep but felt so worried and addled, I didn't see how it could happen. The bottle was there on the nightstand, so I poured myself some.

"Hey, go easy, there," Marilyn said around her toothbrush.

To me the gin smelled like something you'd clean a floor with. The first tiny sip was awful, so I drank the rest down swiftly. It burned and caused my mouth to fill up with saliva. I spit into the wastebasket.

"How can you drink this?" I said.

"I used to only drink it with chocolate cake," she said. "Then one day, I found I didn't need the cake anymore."

I asked her for some raisins. She brought them from her purse along with a key on a plastic tag. "Go next door and go to bed," she said.

54

I thought a stiff drink was supposed to help you sleep, but it only made everything worse for me. I think I slept an hour before I woke up sweating and sick. The mattress seemed to turn like a record on a turntable. The problem of where Betty had gone was like a skip in the record.

I got up and washed my face, then went back to bed and worried. I must have slept some more, too. I dreamed I cracked an egg and a chick was in there, alive. When the sun came past the curtain edge I got up and pounded on Marilyn's door.

She was already dressed, including the zipper boots and fresh makeup. She studied me awhile, then brought me some water in a cup. "Let's go find a pay phone," she said.

I reminded her of the one at the truck stop.

"I'm not supposed to use the same one twice," she said.

We took the Caprice. I went inside a Winn-Dixie grocery store while she made her call. When I came out she had pulled the car up to the Winn-Dixie entrance. She had her big sunglasses on.

"The Main Office isn't happy. We're to stay put while they contact Ray Sloan."

"You told me you're already in contact with Ray," I said.

"There's a protocol. He's still underground, so it'll take some time."

We were waiting while an old man passed in front of us with a six-pack of empty returnable bottles. He was moving very slowly.

"I don't understand what's happening," I said. "Why is Ray still hiding? Can't you just put him somewhere safe?"

"Do you have to understand?"

"Better than I do now, yes."

She seemed to consider what to tell me. We drove. The air conditioner made a low noise. It was much quieter in this car than in the

Scamp, where we rode with the windows down and Betty smacked her gum and fussed with the radio.

"Why did you and Ray leave D.C.?" Marilyn asked.

"Something happened there. I don't know the details."

"You left the morning after the Watergate arrests."

I nodded.

"It's a problem, Angela. Agency people ought not to become involved in something like that. Even former Agency people. It creates an impression that the Agency itself was involved."

"Wasn't it?"

"Of course not. We don't operate on U.S. soil."

"Whose soil are you on right now?"

"What, this? This is not an *operation*," she said. "We're just riding around. I changed your tire."

"Is the Bureau looking for Ray?"

"That is what we're trying to prevent. They've got a full-on manhunt going for this other guy." She mentioned HORSEFLY's name.

"Thank you for helping us," I said.

"You are quite welcome, my dear."

"I'm surprised you gave me a room by myself last night."

"I can't sleep with somebody else in the bed," she said. "Don't tell me you read that rag." She had noticed the new issue of *World News Digest* that I had bought at Winn-Dixie.

"It's for entertainment," I said.

Back at the truck stop my eggs and bacon made me think of Betty again. Or was it something else that caused me to think of her? Through the window I observed a neglected flower bed with some white things in it resembling dirty boat fenders. A brown waif in a pink gingham dress squatted nearby, poking at one of the white things with her finger. Yes, it was Betty.

I ran from my seat, and Marilyn followed close behind.

"Ding!" I said. I threw my arms around her.

"Huh?" She pushed me away.

"What are you doing?"

"Looking at a fungus."

"Ding, meet my Aunt Marilyn." This was the cover story that Marilyn and I had agreed to the previous night, before we had given up looking.

Betty gave Marilyn a look I knew well—the same one she had given me that first time I saw her at the Golden Monkey Restaurant. It was an expression of malign emptiness, dumb and shifty—a cigar-store Indian without the feathers. You couldn't read that look, but it certainly made you feel looked at. It was a treat seeing her give it to someone besides me.

"We waited up for you last night," I said.

"Okay. Look at this big fungus," Betty said.

Marilyn removed her sunglasses to inspect the thing in the flower bed. "What the heck is it, a mushroom?"

There were three the size of basketballs. Even up close they looked like discarded dirty vinyl, until you touched one and saw how easily the surface was scored or torn with a fingernail. I did not touch one myself, because I once had a bad reaction after handling a mushroom, but I watched Betty do it.

"I think these are puffballs," Marilyn said.

"Hey, Ding, did you hear me say that Marilyn is my aunt? Where have you been?"

"Walk around, mostly."

"We heard you went off with a trucker named Skeet."

She wouldn't say. She stood there nudging a puffball with the toe of her white tennis shoe.

"Well, food is on the table," Marilyn said. "Have you eaten?"

"No."

We ordered more eggs, more bacon. I hoped Betty would use the spoon on her eggs again, so Marilyn could see it. But she used a fork this time.

Afterward Marilyn lit a cigarette. Betty tipped her head at the pack. "Maybe I will join you."

Marilyn shook a long Marlboro out. Betty turned it in her fingers, examining. Would she accept it? Did it meet her high standard for freebies? I had given her that hundred dollars, but I had yet to see her pay for anything. Even at Sears she had acted strangely in the checkout line, sending me off while she waited.

Finally she placed Marilyn's cigarette in her mouth. "I have start to like American cigarette," she said.

For a follower of Chairman Mao she behaved awfully like a princess at times. And yet I was so relieved to have her back in hand, her bad qualities didn't bother me like they used to. I tolerated her pretty well now.

55

"You know this girl's father?" Betty asked Marilyn.

"I'm her aunt," Marilyn said.

"What name do you call her?"

Marilyn took a long last draw on her cigarette before mashing it out. "*Pumpkin.*"

"Mm." Betty tamped out her cigarette carefully and hid what remained of it (about half) somewhere on her person. Whatever Betty wore, it always seemed to have some hidden pockets in it, because she was constantly producing some item you didn't know she had or else making something disappear, and she didn't carry a bag of any kind.

"I could use a shower," I said.

We went back to the Crown Motor Court, where I was able to have a go at Betty in private.

"What about this Skeet you left with?" I said.

She claimed she had gotten as far as the cab of his truck before he showed her some unwelcome attentions and she hopped back out.

"What did you think he was going to do, braid your hair?"

"I thought he will do what he did, probably. But I thought it will be worth a try. My friend has left me."

"I came back! We waited half the night for you."

She gave a dry sniff and drew her knees up to her chest. She was on my bed, looking at the television, which was off.

"I can't explain," I said.

"I don't ask you to explain."

I went into the shower. When I came out I found her staring into the Gideon Bible. She had discovered the pages reproducing various languages of the world, including her own, I suppose.

"I do not understand Jesus," she said.

"That's because you're a Communist."

This room was a good deal nicer than the one at the King's Way with bedbugs. The bed was a double, and there were two chairs. I sat down on the one facing Betty and asked where she had spent the night.

"In truck."

"I thought you ran off after Skeet touched you."

"Different truck. Forget it."

I didn't forget it, but I put it aside. "I have to tell you something about Marilyn," I said.

"Tell."

I told her that Marilyn was my secret aunt—an aunt on my father's side that my mother didn't know about. "That should explain why we have to meet in private like this."

"Unusual story."

"It's not really that my mother doesn't *know* about her. My mother hates her, you see, and we are forbidden to visit. It all goes back to a boy they fought over, many years ago."

"The fought over your father?"

"No. Never mind." I could never tell what Betty believed or didn't.

"Your aunt is not very happy or relax," Betty said.

"These secretive meetings make her nervous."

"Way she smoke and eat, seem like she hate herself."

"I don't know how you could tell something like that after eating breakfast with her one time."

"Easy to tell. Way she smoke cigarette, way she sit, don't eat much, pinch her arm. Not happy. I got a aunt just like her."

"Her work is stressful," I said.

"What work?"

"She's studying to be a park ranger."

"Not stressful." Betty went to the sink and loudly rinsed her mouth out. She came back to the bed.

"So Betty has an aunt," I said. "That's the first you have mentioned of any relatives."

"Everybody has got some relatives."

"Do you miss this aunt?"

"Only miss my old parents," she said.

Suddenly she had a small paper packet in her fingers. She tore it open and sprinkled black pepper into her palm, and she began eating the pepper with the point of her tongue.

56

The hot day crept by, broken only by a walk along U.S. 11, the highlight of which was when Betty saw two garter snakes lying together and jumped sideways over a ditch. It was a wide ditch and she landed running. If I had known she was afraid of snakes I would not have pointed them out to her. Now it was evening, and Betty was lying down in our room. Marilyn went off alone to visit another pay phone, then asked me into her room to talk.

"Do you think Ding accepts the Aunt Marilyn story?" Marilyn asked.

"She's practical-minded," I said. "She'll go along with it until she has a reason not to."

"All right. I need you to do something, Angela."

"What's that?"

"I need you to signal Ray. Call him in."

"Why don't *you* call him in?"

"He's not responding. You have a way to signal him, right?"

I didn't answer.

She sat on the edge of the dresser. Two lamps were on, and the curtains were pulled. From her large purse she unfolded a copy of the *World News Digest*. "I tried the crossword," she said. "It's too easy. There is an interesting set of personal ads in the back, however. Here's one signed *Boney Maroney*."

"I'm not Boney Maroney."

"I know, I already talked to her. She's a high school band director in Indianapolis. And she's a man."

Marilyn poured herself a cup of gin.

"You are going to have to trust me, Angela."

"I have trusted you," I said. "I'm here, aren't I? I could have left at any time."

"No. If you leave I will quickly find you again. The reason is, *I don't work alone.* Nobody does in this trade. We're a machine, and we have to trust each other. Working alone is how you ball things up. It's poor tradecraft. Believe me on this, because I know."

She began to pace and lecture me. I was risking my life and Ray's by not cooperating fully, she claimed. I thought I knew everything because I had partly grown up at the Farm, but in fact I was only a precocious child who had read a few spy books. I did not understand the real methods of clandestine work as it is practiced in the field, she said. "You're *fourteen*! You're driving through mountains without sleep in a car registered to Ray Sloan, and you're not even a legal driver. And Betty!"

Our eyes met and she looked away from me.

"I'm sorry to be rough, Angela. It amazes me you've gotten this far. People always seem to be looking past you."

"People look past me because I have no value to them."

"But now you do have value. You're Ray's vulnerability."

57

ME: How do you figure that?

MARILYN: I don't need to spell it out, do I?

ME: Yes.

MARILYN: Maybe I should start by explaining to you how an Agency cover works.

ME: I think I know, but go ahead.

MARILYN: First of all, an Agency cover is known to a number of people. Your supervisor knows, and so does his supervisor. It's all written down. Some friends in the Agency will know about it, too. An Agency cover is not a secret that is kept only in your bosom. If you have secrets that are only known to you and Ray, then those are not Agency secrets, Angela. They're just secrets. They might even be secrets *from* the Agency. Do you understand?

ME: No.

MARILYN: Second. We might live an elaborate cover overseas, but not at home. We don't run around D.C. using false names and false passports. The Agency would not send a girl to public school with a false birth certificate.

ME: Come to the point.

MARILYN: The point is that Ray has been hiding something.

ME: What?

She handed me a stiff, glossy snapshot. At first I did not recognize anyone in it. The woman's hair was covered with a scarf, and she was laughing. Her teeth were a bright blur. She looked happy and rather glamorous. The man wore a light suit and sunglasses and held a baby.

MARILYN: Who are those people?

ME: I don't know. You tell me.

MARILYN: Well, there's Ray Sloan, looking quite a bit younger and more dashing than the Ray we know. And according to the file, he's with his late wife, Celeste, and their daughter Angela. Which would be you, correct?

ME: Babies all look the same to me.

MARILYN: You'd recognize your own mother, though.

ME: She died a long time ago.

MARILYN: How old were you?

ME: I forget.

MARILYN: That's a lie. You can't have forgotten how old you were when your mother died.

ME: I was seven.

MARILYN: The girl in this picture was four years old when her mother was killed. She would be twelve now. You're fourteen, right? About to turn fifteen?

ME: A lot of people were killed in Stanleyville. Some of them don't have files.

MARILYN: What are you talking about?

ME: I'm saying not everyone in the universe has a file somewhere. Some people are born and live and their names are never typed onto a form.

MARILYN: Has Ray been decent with you?

ME: Of course he's been decent with me.

MARILYN: Not "of course." He has or he hasn't, but it could be either way.

ME: He took me in after my family was murdered.

MARILYN: Has he ever used you like a girlfriend?

ME: No. You're disgusting.

MARILYN: It's an unusual arrangement that you two have. He told his chief of station that you were his daughter. Lying to the C.O.S. is not considered good. Why would he do that?

ME: Maybe it was the only way he could keep me.

MARILYN: It's true, the Agency doesn't encourage its officers to adopt foreign orphans.

ME: There's your explanation, then.

MARILYN: But why would he want to keep you?

ME: I don't know.

MARILYN: Is there something Ray feels guilty about?

ME: Like what?

MARILYN: Are you aware how his wife died?

ME: No.

MARILYN: The Simbas made a spectacle of it. They were—

ME: I don't need to hear it.

MARILYN: We think the child died in a similar way. What about your parents?

ME: What about them?

MARILYN: What *happened* to them?

ME: Simbas killed them.

MARILYN: What's your real name?

ME: Stop it!

MARILYN: You probably have relatives somewhere.

ME: Everybody has got some relatives somewhere.

MARILYN: There is no need for all of this to be buried, Angela. This is extraordinary. It isn't normal.

ME: Ray is my family. He's the one who took me in.

MARILYN: Did Ray have something to do with what happened to your parents?

ME: Of course not. What do you mean?

MARILYN: I'm asking whether your parents were involved with Ray. Were they part of his network?

ME: I was seven!

MARILYN: Okay. You wouldn't know.

ME: You have got everything backwards and inside out.

MARILYN: Maybe so. It was a rocky operation in Stanleyville—no local contacts, and most of it was off the books. Ray's network is something of a legend, though. He had these beer trucks traveling all over rebel-held territory. The Simbas were devoted to beer, so the trucks always got through. That's how we found Che Guevara there. One of Ray's drivers heard about a white man training rebels in the bush. Che was trying to teach them French, apparently. So they could be *politicized*. What a plan. I'll tell you this: Ray Sloan was a first-rate operator in his

day. I guess he just lost it when they killed his family. Under-
standable. He certainly earned his downtime at Camp Peary.

ME: He was a valued instructor there.

MARILYN: Right.

ME: Are you implying that he was put out to pasture?

MARILYN: Did you ever wonder why they call it the Farm? Anyway, call him in. We'll get it straightened out. We'll get you
set up, too, Angela. I've seen the birth certificate you gave the
D.C. school system. What did you do, make it yourself?

ME: It worked.

MARILYN: But it won't work your whole life. Suppose you want to
get married someday.

ME: Give me a break.

MARILYN: Suppose you want to work for the post office. You're
going to need a sure enough birth certificate. Can you call Ray
tonight?

ME: No. It'll take a few days.

MARILYN: You should not have chosen a weekly paper for your
method of communicating.

ME: I'll make the call in the morning, at nine.

MARILYN: Nine it is. Where's Ding?

ME: I think she's sleeping.

MARILYN: You should do the same. We'll talk tomorrow. Go to
bed.

She turned her back to me, refilling her cup.

58

I don't know why I hadn't expected Ray's wife to be so beautiful. She had dark eyes and that gorgeous, careless smile. Ray wore the smallest grin on his mouth, as though he were trying to contain it. He held the baby tightly in both arms.

I was sitting on the curb outside Marilyn's room. I studied the picture, which she had neglected to take back from me.

Why did it surprise me that Celeste was so attractive? Ray was a nice-looking man. It was hard to imagine him keeping a glamorous woman entertained, though. The Ray I knew was not a conversationalist, and he didn't attend parties. He wore the same shirt two days in a row. He would wear a pair of pants until something got on them.

It never had occurred to me before this moment that I had not known Ray at his best. What a disappointment it must have been to him, to lose this wife and the child who would have resembled her in many ways. *Disappointment* is not an adequate word, but I don't know what other word to use. The disappointed Ray was the only Ray I'd ever known.

Why had he wanted to keep me? At such great risk? I couldn't imagine why. I was no beauty. My personality was something less than scintillating. Maybe he'd kept me just because I insisted. After losing everything, I clung to him.

I remembered my own mother well. I had a stock of memories and went through them often enough. My mother was sturdy, not glamorous. She had brown hair and only sometimes trimmed the very ends. She wore it up, but I remember her bathing me with her hair down and color in her face from the heat. Each memory was something trivial, yet they glowed for me in a strange way. I remembered my father shouting at her in the kitchen; my mother crying; my mother with a pencil behind her ear; my father running into a storm to grab a goat that was loose from its pen. He did that for me, because I was afraid the goat would be struck by lightning. My father was good, though he did shout sometimes.

I found myself sitting there crying on the curb outside the motel rooms, crying because my life was so wrong and backward. I was this hard thing—this clipping or scrap of a person. I would never be normal.

None of that matters to anyone but me. I mention these thoughts only because they came to me at this crucial time. I was about to make a step. I must make the call and place the ad to ask Ray to come back to me. It was against his instructions but I was relieved to have a need to do it because I was worried about him. I only had one question to answer first.

I got up and pushed into Room 9. There was Betty, cutting an apple with Ray's yellow-handled pocketknife. I snatched it away from her. "Where did you find this?" I said.

"On the ground."

On inspection I saw it was not Ray's knife but a similar, cheaper one with a stainless steel blade. I gave Betty's apple knife back to her.

"Listen," I said. "I know you've been talking to my Aunt Marilyn when I'm not around."

"No, I have not talk to her. What is that?" She meant the snapshot in my hand.

"It's nothing."

She took the picture and studied it. "Is this your father?"

"Give it back!" I grabbed her wrist in order to take the picture back. I got it.

She pulled free. She went into the bathroom, shutting the door and locking it behind her.

At the door I said, "You've talked to Marilyn in private. I know you have. She knows your name. I heard her call you Betty."

Silence.

"I was stupid to trust you," I said. "I tried to get you papers so you wouldn't be deported, and now you have lied to me about Marilyn. You may even be working for her. I suppose you are. You are a liar."

The door unlocked and came open one half inch. "I have never talk to Aunt Marilyn alone," Betty said.

The door closed again.

59

That couldn't be true. Marilyn *had* called her Betty; I'd heard it. I'd been careful only to use the name Ding with Marilyn.

I was standing there by the motel sink outside the bathroom door when it occurred to me what had happened. Blood rushed to my skin. I had been very stupid.

It wasn't Betty who was working with Marilyn, it was the Gandys. After leaving their house I had driven all night through the mountains. I'd have been easy to find, easy to tail. In the morning, Marilyn changed my tire (after putting the nail in it herself, no doubt). Then she followed close so I would detect her. I had given myself the credit for making her, just like she meant for me to do. I let her *develop* me, in my state of crazed exhaustion. I was seeing old ladies in the road; then here came Marilyn with her war stories. She'd "lost an asset." I was sucked in and quickly *involved*. She showed me that snapshot and fed me a lot of lies and bogus hints about Ray Sloan. "Is there something Ray feels guilty about?" What a poor sucker I had been. Nothing but a poor sucker. If not for the one slip on Betty's name, Marilyn would have turned me.

I saw it now. I had almost been *doubled*. The way Marilyn did it was to make me wonder who I was. Was I real? But it didn't matter. Ray was real: he was out there, alone and maybe sick, and I could still be true to him. *Idaho meant bug out.*

Now I knew what I had to do. I tucked the stiff snapshot away. I slid it down in the brown envelope which also held my nine remaining hundreds.

It meant leaving Betty behind for good. The thought didn't please me. In spite of her foreign manners and Communist beliefs, she had been a companion to me. I'd put some time and energy into her, and I didn't like leaving her in Marilyn's hands. Marilyn would not indulge her with shopping and gum as I had done. In the future, Betty would find herself doing as told, and it would cause her some pain. On the other hand, if her story about the party-official boyfriend convinced the right people, she'd get asylum and a legal set of papers. She could work anywhere, then. Even her dreamland of Sears and Roebuck.

As I tucked the brown envelope back into my knapsack, I kept out one of the hundreds. I slipped it into a pocket of Betty's black pants.

Just as I was doing this charitable deed she popped out of the bathroom. There was no warning flush, as she'd been in there only hanging out, a trick she had borrowed from me. My hand was in her pocket.

She snatched the black pants and gave them a close looking-over. She even smelled them.

"What are you up to?" she said.

60

"Four-foot-ten," I said.

She blinked. "Why will you handle my pants?"

"I was looking for a quarter for the candy machine."

"You have put one hundred dollars in here."

"I don't like to keep all our cash in one place," I said. "That's not smart, in case my knapsack gets stolen." I held it up by the strap for her to see—my knapsack with the sunflowers on it. It was a good lie and would have worked, had I not already told her the other lie about the candy machine.

Yet she accepted what I said with a nod. She folded the pants and set them back on the dresser where they had been. They were clean— she had rinsed the lake water out and dried them on the shower rod. The white blouse was draped over the chair back, also clean. Betty sat on the edge of the bed and held her green hairbrush.

I got on my side of the bed with my back against the headboard and my black oxfords on. I had the knapsack on the floor nearby. All I had to do was wait for Betty to get to sleep, and then I'd slip out the door. Marilyn was into her gin; she'd be asleep soon, too, if not already. If I didn't get lost I could be in Bristol and on the new expressway in under an hour; I'd abandon the Scamp in Virginia and would be on a Greyhound bus before Marilyn knew I was gone.

Betty held the brush in her lap. I asked her if she wanted the television on.

"No." She laid the brush on the nightstand and got under the covers.

"No brush hair tonight?"

"My hair is not important," she said.

"Nobody's hair is important in the long run of things," I said.

I took my shoes off and laid them together on the floor beside the bed, where I could get into them quickly in the dark. I faked a yawn. "I'm so sleepy I could fall asleep just like this, right in my clothes on top of the bedspread."

Betty said nothing.

"Time for lights out," I said. I switched off the lamp.

"Goodbye," Betty said.

I sat up and switched the lamp back on.

Betty lay there like a small angry mummy. Her eyes were open, fixed on the ceiling.

"I don't owe you anything, by the way," I said. "You're in your box and I'm in mine. Anyway, Marilyn's not after you, she's after me."

"She is after you?"

"She wants something I have. So I'm leaving."

"You are going to take Scamp?"

"How am I going to leave if I don't take Scamp?"

Betty pursed her mouth. Otherwise her brown face was still amid the black hair spread out on the pillow.

"You're using that Oriental trick again, but it won't work," I said. I swung my legs down from the bed and put on my shoes.

"What do you mean, Oriental trick?"

"You lie there inscrutably refusing to speak, and it is a trick for causing me to have the argument inside my head instead of out loud."

"I don't know about that," she said.

"Let me demonstrate," I said. I came close to her. She was propped on her elbow now, and I got eight inches away and let all the expression drain from my face as I stared at a spot on her cheek. "Look, you can't read me," I said. "I'm inscrutable, I'm a cipher. I'm a crustacean."

"Stop it."

"That's what you're like! Always making me guess what you think."

"What do you guess I think?"

"Oh, you're thinking you are going to be alone, you have no Chinese friend, you can't make revolution, you're a snake in a hole."

"So. I am *not* inscrutable."

She smiled a sour smile that dimpled her chin. She seemed to think she had won the point.

I got up and gave my teeth a good long noisy scrubbing, followed by a vigorous rinse and spit. After that I went back to Betty and told her she should not feel all of this so much. "Though miles and an ocean separate you, you are still with your Chinese people in spirit."

"You are right," she said. "I will try not to feel it so much."

She smiled again, strangely. The look was strange because it suddenly seemed unmysterious, like the way a friend would smile at you if something sad were happening. It confused me.

"I knew something was wrong when you didn't brush your hair," I said.

She took the brush from the nightstand and gave her head a good, fierce working over. At last, the shiny hair received its nightly spanking. When she was done she pulled a couple of long loose strands from the bristles and walked across the room to drop them in the wastebasket.

Ten minutes earlier I had known what I was doing, and now I did not know again.

"Why don't you give me back that hundred and just come with me?" I said.

I returned the crisp bill to the envelope. Betty gathered her few things quietly, and we slipped out of Room 9 together.

61

The engine heaved but didn't catch. Out of nervousness I had pumped the gas, once again flooding the carburetor.

"Is that your uncle?" Betty asked.

The door to Marilyn's room had swung open, and a man stood staring at us. But no, it wasn't a man, only Marilyn with her hair wet and dressed in a man's set of striped pajamas. The cuffs were rolled up at her ankles and wrists. I flattened the accelerator and twisted the key, the engine roared, and we reversed through our own smoke across the parking lot.

Goodbye, Crown Motor Court. I sideswiped a light pole. Betty groaned. "What will happen to me?" she said.

"Now is a time to be quiet," I said.

"What?"

"Stay out of my head!"

The white Caprice came after us and caught us at a red light. Marilyn got out in her pajamas and jogged to my window. "Let's talk, Angela!" she said. "Let me in!"

I ran the light.

"I will be arrest and deport," Betty said. "I will be send back to China and put in jail. Then confess, then execute. Very unpleasant to be execute, girl! Let me out of this Scamp!"

"Aunt Marilyn's very drunk," I said. "I think we can lose her."

In fact she was soon in front of us. She slowed way down, swerving when I tried to pass. The Scamp had served me well up to now, but it didn't have the power to get around Marilyn's Chevy Caprice. Nor was I the driver to do it.

Betty was shouting in Chinese. Well, here it is, I thought. This is the moment of crisis. Now what? We crossed a river on a narrow two-lane bridge with low rails. Marilyn rode her brakes in front of us. We were going no more than thirty miles an hour when a third car came up fast behind me and had to burn its tires to stay out of my bumper.

The driver behind me leaned on his horn. As soon as we were off the bridge, I switched off my headlights and whipped the Scamp to the right. The angry fellow quickly closed the gap, helpfully flashing his high beams in Marilyn's rearview mirror.

With my lights still off, I turned back the way we had come. There was half a moon tonight, enough for me to see by. I crossed back over the river to where some orange sawhorses were lined up along the road. I edged the Scamp past the sawhorses and drove it over some rutted clay.

"Where are we go?" Betty said.

I stopped the car.

A number of trees had been pushed over intact beside the road, and the big machines that do that kind of thing were parked nearby. The trees lay on the clay with boulders knotted in their roots.

I told her what I intended to do.

"Bad idea," she said.

"It's my only idea," I said. "Help me."

"Bad idea. We will try."

I found the biggest rock I could lift and heaved it into the back seat.

Behind the wheel again, I punched the gas. The new tires spun, then grabbed. I covered a long stretch of rough ground, then pulled the wheel and bumped up three inches onto a new slab of rich, creamy-smooth black asphalt pavement. I was on the new road.

It felt like driving on sheets of cake. We were traveling north now over what would later become the southbound lanes of Interstate 81. If you will check the 1972 Esso map of the eastern United States, you will see this stretch marked by a heavy broken red and white line—one of the last gaps remaining to be paved on the long route down from Canada through Syracuse, Scranton, and the Shenandoah Valley into East Tennessee.

It was a great big open night. For the moment, Betty and I drove in perfect, blank solitude. The tires whispered against the new surface. The lines were not even painted on it yet. The good Scamp gave what I asked of it. Its transmission clicked up into third gear, and the sound of the engine evened out.

An orange cone marked the beginning of the bridge deck. I'd expected something more substantial than one orange cone, but no. I simply drove around it, then I stopped and put the Scamp in park.

Betty and I got out and stood awhile. There was no sign of Marilyn, and yet I felt as though someone were watching us. I guess Betty felt it, too. "Strange time," she said. We were alone at the edge of an unfinished bridge, a hundred feet over the Holston River, at night. Many unfinished thoughts were in my head. I guess no one was watching.

Well off in the distance we saw long cones of light bouncing over the ground. I knew she'd be along.

I took off one of my thick-soled black oxford shoes and jammed it behind the Scamp's brake pedal. Then I pushed my sunflower knapsack down onto the floor. I wadded a towel and my Toughskins and a map and shoved them down in front of the seat to form a little nest on top of the accelerator. I did it quickly. Then I dropped that big rock into its nest, causing the engine to rev.

Only then did I remember the brown envelope. And the picture. So stupid! I bent to get it. The knapsack was at the bottom, flap side down, and my arms were shaking. Betty was screaming something. There wasn't time.

"Marilyn will see you!" Betty said.

I had to let something go, so I gave up the envelope. I pushed down on the rock. The engine raced.

Marilyn's headlights bounced. From the driver's-side door, I jerked the gearshift lever. The car jumped, veering toward me. I pushed the steering wheel to straighten it. Betty had my arm. She tore me free of the car, and we bolted, me in my one shoe.

The Caprice's headlights lit the Scamp as the Scamp cruised over the edge of the bridge deck. It didn't go straight off. It hit the edge at an angle, bottomed out, scraped, and tipped and went over, out of sight. The engine ran away and whined. There was a long, slow crash when the car hit the water.

Marilyn stopped. She walked up ahead of the Caprice and stood in her headlights in her men's pajamas. Betty and I lay flat behind a bundle of steel bars. Marilyn wasn't looking for us, though. She thought she knew where we were.

Pretty soon she left. Betty and I ran off into the darkness, and that was when something hit me in the face.

62

Betty ran on some ways until she noticed I wasn't with her any-more. Upon coming back to me, she claims, she found me lying stone dead with my hair full of warm blood under the scoop of a front-end loader. She pounded on my chest until my heart began to "walk" again, as she put it. She placed my limp body over her shoulder and carried me several miles along the side of a rocky hill in the dark.

She washed my face and hair in a hole of dirty water. I revived. She then persuaded a garbage man to drive us to North Carolina in his garbage truck.

I have no memory of any of that, so I can't vouch for how she got us to North Carolina. She did it somehow. As for my having died and come back, I would say that she imagined or made that part up, except for one thing. When I finally did come to—I mean when I was able to look around myself and see that I was in the woods, barefooted now and wearing someone else's dress—there was one thing missing from my head, and that was my usually reliable sense of how long I had been asleep. It was not like waking up. It was more like starting from Go.

I was thirsty and confused. When I closed my eyes, my mother's plain, kind face seemed to hover in my brain, and I remembered her singing and gently scolding me.

Then I thought of the picture of Ray with his daughter and wife that I had lost, and I sat up. Everything came back to me now, and I couldn't believe I had been so stupid. All my money was gone as well.

The loss of the money was serious, and yet it was the loss of those people in the picture that discouraged me more. How could I ever tell Ray what I'd done? I had no right to lose the last trace of them.

I recalled the family set of stolen driver's licenses that I had seen at Lucky Bus Tour. Those sad, smiling faces. It made me feel bleak.

Names can float off one way, faces another. People can just get lost. Most people will be remembered a little while, not long.

I lay like a rug in the dappled, humid spot in the woods where Betty had put me.

A creek muttered nearby. At my side I had a hump of mossy limestone. Below the leaves, the black soil had cottony white tendrils in it, tiny red mites, and bits of sparkling mica. A blotch of sunlight crept up my leg. I watched it go.

There was nothing to do but slowly eat the time. I thought of Ray Sloan on surveillance and surveillance detection drills in Newport News and Williamsburg. In a parked car with his elbow out the window and a cigarette burning in his fingers, he remained still for so long that he sometimes resembled a mannequin.

The use of being still, he told me once, is that there is a range of things you will never see, until the rustle of your most recent movement has completely dissipated. "The first half hour doesn't count," he said.

It was true. I was staring at a mound of violets by my leg when I saw that the thing just behind them was a box turtle. It had a yellow rim around its eye.

Another hour went.

A dark bird the size of a duck or a little bigger swooped in and took a short, clumsy walk along the creek. Its bill was sharp, and its curving neck was as long as its body. A black crest pointed backward from its head. I have since looked it up: it was the *Butorides striatus* or green heron.

To avoid confusion it is better to learn a creature's Latin name when you can. For example, the bird called a redstart in England is the *Phoenicurus phoenicurus,* but the bird we call a redstart over here is a *Setophaga ruticilla.* Two different birds.

I like to keep things straight like that, though I suppose it doesn't matter to the bird what you call it, no more than it matters to the dead person when at last his name has floated away. It doesn't matter, does it? I'll remember while I'm alive. The world will carry on. I don't really think I died this time, but if so, dying was not so awfully bad.

ays passed. Betty fed me from cans of deviled ham, tuna, and fruit cocktail. When I asked for something different, she left and came back with a can of potato sticks and a fresh pear. She also brought me some jeans, a Western-style shirt with snaps, and tennis shoes. I asked Betty how much cash she had left.

"Hundred dollar."

"That can't be right," I said. "I took back that hundred at the motel the other night, so it's gone now. How did you get all the food and these clothes?"

"Stole."

"Wait a minute. Are you talking about the hundred I gave you at the lake? I thought you broke it buying clothes at the Sears in Knoxville."

"I stole!"

"You walked out of Sears without paying?"

"Mm."

I contemplated her. As I've said, there wasn't much to her—just a wiry brown Chinese girl who looked like she wouldn't mind fighting. Some people are that way, and it has nothing to do with being Oriental or not. Her hands were black because she'd been scraping mud off an enamel pot that she'd pulled from the creek. It made me sad and frustrated to think she would salvage a dirty chipped pot when there were a hundred U.S. dollars tucked away in one of those secret pockets.

"I worry about you stealing things, Betty," I said. "That's not how we do it here! Get caught, and it causes me all kinds of problems. Now you're stealing potato sticks. The whole can costs twenty-seven cents! You're an illegal alien. Just pay for the can!"

"I never will be bother by police. Only have to be a little smart."

"I know you are a little smart. I'm talking about best practices."

"You do not trust me," she said. "You are bad to me. I am very angry now. Maybe I will leave you alone in this wilderness." She threw some leaves on me.

"Don't do that. I'm sorry," I said.

"Not enough! Not enough."

"What do you want me to do?"

She barked something, climbed over a fallen tree trunk, and stomped away.

It was time for us to move along. I knew something about Betty that Betty didn't know: namely, a meal in a restaurant would do her a world of good. At her best she was no Mary Poppins, but the grouchiness had hit a new extreme here in the woods. I also had begun to form a notion in my mind about heading south to Florida. Why not? My next idea was a change in our appearances.

I got on my feet. I could walk okay. That afternoon, Betty and I walked into the town of Singleton, North Carolina. It wasn't much, just a couple dozen storefronts along Main Street. You could take the whole place in with a turn of your head. A man with a beard like a dirty hand towel winked at me on the sidewalk.

I checked a paper in the door of a newspaper machine. It was the third of July, a Monday, and the hairstylist's shop was closed. An establishment called Beauty's Light Touch Grooming was open for business, however. I told the lady what I wanted.

"This is a dog-grooming establishment," the lady said. "I don't do girls' hair."

"But you could."

"It doesn't work that way, dear."

The drugstore next door had a delightful smell coming out of it. "Let's go in here and break that hundred," I said. We took a pair of stools at the counter. "I am getting a grilled cheese with onions on it, and I want you to order whatever you like," I told Betty. She chose a ham sandwich.

If you have ever watched a cat enjoy a ham sandwich, that was how Betty ate hers, too. She flipped the bread over and devoured the ham from inside, then picked at the lettuce and the tomato slice. I saw her forehead become smooth again. I noted, too, that she was one of these people who raise their eyebrows when taking a bite. I was getting to know old Betty pretty well.

The onions on my grilled cheese sandwich were finely minced. The bread had been grilled rather dark, per my request. I was so pleased with my sandwich and with myself for thinking of it that I hardly noticed the tall boy sliding his sandals over the dusty tile until, by accident, our eyes met. It was Eeyore! He looked away shyly, giving no sign of having recognized me. He slouched away to the register, where he paid for a wind-up alarm clock and carried it out of the drugstore in a paper bag.

I thought we were okay. Betty fed with her face two inches from the plate, so maybe he hadn't noticed her. My own face was nothing memorable, I supposed. Then someone cried out, "Ding!"

It was Renee. She ran toward us, hurling a smile ahead of her.

was very suspicious, and I nearly came right out and asked Renee, "Who has sent you after us?" But before I could get the question out she clapped both her arms around me.

"I've got friends everywhere!" she proclaimed.

We were on the sidewalk now—Renee, old long Eeyore in his sandal shoon, Betty/Ding, and me, whom Renee kept calling Lucy, since that was the name I had told her back in Knoxville, evidently.

"Why are you here?" I said.

"I don't know!" she said. She laughed in her high-spirited way, and even Eeyore couldn't help smiling, though he tried not to. Then Renee spun and gave her hair a great flick so that it flew out in a platter shape with the sun pouring over it. Honestly, she was quite a specimen. She caught the eye of the man with the hand-towel beard.

"You're pretty," he said.

"*Thanks,*" Renee answered politely.

He worked his hands rapidly one against the other, as though he were knitting. He was dressed in crusty jeans and four flannel shirts. "You sure are pretty," he said.

Eeyore squirmed. He was a foot and a half taller than the other man but lacked his intensity. "We better go," Eeyore said.

"Will you and Ding come meet our friends?" Renee asked me.

"Yes," the man with the beard said.

I asked her who her friends were.

"Dirk and Wilhelmina."

Confused, I agreed. We climbed into a white van, all of us but the "You're pretty" man. "I'm sorry you can't come with us," Renee told him.

"Why can't I come with you, pretty girl?"

"Eeyore doesn't want you to."

It caused Renee real pain to disappoint this fellow. He called, "Good-bye, goodbye!" and she blew him kisses out the front passenger window as Eeyore drove us away.

It was a Ford cargo van. The interior had been furnished in the style of a hippie sitting room, with shell beads in the windows, a short daybed, and a fan-backed wicker garden chair that slid freely over the steel deck. It smelled like old laundry and leaf smoke in there.

"Nice van," I said.

"It's Dirk and Wilhelmina's," Renee said. "But Dirk doesn't like to drive. He and Wilhelmina live *an ascetic lifestyle.*"

"Is that right?"

"You will like Wilhelmina. Everything she says is super gassy."

"Where am I going?" Betty said.

That was the first she had spoken since we'd left the drugstore. Renee turned in her seat to look, and only then did the whole business come back to me about Ding not knowing English.

"*Bless you!*" I said to Betty.

Renee blinked at me.

"*Gesundheit,*" Eeyore said.

65

Five or six miles out of town, Eeyore stopped to let Renee open a gate. We struggled another half mile in first gear along two uneven ruts between drooping hemlock branches. The track opened into a clearing with a funny cottage made of salvage in the middle of it.

One end of the cottage was covered in clapboard with the bark still on, the other clad in roof metal. The covered porch was built of sticks. The whole thing had been painted red like a barn.

The roof was tiled with overlapping squares of green and white linoleum. A porcelain bathtub had caught some rainwater under the gutterless eaves. In the yard a two-seater bicycle lay on its side with grass growing up through the spokes.

Somewhere out of sight, a shrill male voice complained. A second voice answered, cool, sharp, and female. Renee popped her eyes at me. "Sometimes they get pretty cross with each other," she whispered.

As we came around the corner of the cottage we saw a woman in muddy fatigue pants and a muddy black turtleneck. She stood facing a bush. Perhaps it wasn't so much a bush as a hump of leaves and brush, like when a fence post has grown over with honeysuckle. "Your elbows are sticking out," she said to the bush or hump. She kicked it with her boot, and the hump of brush bounced before it was still again.

Renee called out hello, and the woman turned suddenly. She looked hard at Betty, then at me.

Renee had grabbed our hands. "Wilhelmina, this is Lucy! And this is Ding. We met them last week in Knoxville, and then we ran into them again! Isn't it funny?"

The woman's dark hair was parted in the middle and combed down flat on either side of a very broad, hard-looking white forehead. Her eyes were like little sharp knuckles.

After raking us with her eyes a good while, Wilhelmina strode into the red cottage, knocking aside a cloudy shower curtain that hung in the doorway in place of a door.

The bush stood up on a pair of naked human legs. It followed Wilhelmina inside.

"Wilhelmina doesn't mean to be unkind," Renee said. "She is following a narrow path."

But I felt that a load had been lifted off my mind. These people were too disorganized to be working for the Agency or FBI. My faith in accidents was restored.

Eeyore began to come out of his shell. He asked me to translate a greeting for him, and I could not think how to say no.

"Hello!" he said with a long grin.

I made a noise at Betty, and she replied with something indescribable.

"She says hello back."

"Tell her I ask, 'Are you a Buddhist?'"

More gobbledygook from me, and then Betty used a few phrases that I seemed to recognize from her previous angry soliloquies, like the one in the lake outside Baltimore.

"'My stomach hurts,'" I said.

"Does she want a sandwich?" Renee said.

I answered no for Betty. Betty took a seat away from us, cross-legged on the ground, while at a picnic table Renee made sandwiches of white bread and margarine. She had some sugar packets, too, and for each sandwich she tore a couple open and emptied them on top of the margarine.

"I have never seen this kind of sandwich before," I said.

Dirk and Wilhelmina must have been watching from behind the shower curtain. Like a couple of housecats at the sound of the can opener, they reemerged as the sandwiches were being laid out. Dirk was out of his shrubbery now and had put on some pin-striped trousers and nothing else. He was a lean, pale fellow about five and a half feet tall, compact and nearly hairless except for his head. He ate like a hungry child, staring. Wilhelmina tore off half her sandwich at one bite. When it was gone, she whispered something to Renee, who whispered something to Eeyore, who went to the van and brought back his brown sack from the drugstore. Wilhelmina took the sack and she and Dirk were gone again.

Eeyore produced a set of dominoes. Betty brightened up very slightly at the sight of these and helped to turn them facedown on the picnic table. I was bored out of my skull. A deer poked its head out of the woods. Renee and I went for a walk.

There was something special about Renee and Eeyore that allowed them to accept just about anything they were told. When Renee asked where Ding and I were staying, I told her the truth, that we'd been sleeping in the woods. She said that was beautiful, and that ended it. She had a way of wondering at things without quite managing to form a pertinent question, such as "*Why* are you sleeping in the woods?" In her world, kids did not need reasons. She told me how she and Eeyore had come upon Dirk and Wilhelmina as the latter were being chased from a fruit stand. Renee gave them some Funyuns, and Dirk showed Eeyore how to build a pigeon trap.

"So you're living in this doorless cottage now," I said.

"We didn't mean to come this far," Renee said. "School's out, and Eeyore likes to drive. I'm sure you and Ding are welcome to stay. You can join our study group."

"What are you studying?"

"It depends who is leading the group. We take turns."

"It is kind of you to offer, and I think we will take you up on that," I said.

66

Dirk piled wood for a campfire, but it wouldn't burn. When he'd gone through one book of matches Wilhelmina sent him into the cottage for his "gilly suit." That was what they called his outfit made of brush. He arranged it under some logs, and it went up in a smoky and noisy display. Renee made supper. There we all were, a bunch of soiled hippies by the campfire eating butter and sugar sandwiches.

"Time for study group," Eeyore said.

It was Wilhelmina's turn to lead. "First let's hear from the new people," she said, turning to Betty. "What is your name, sister?"

"That is Ding," I said.

"Where are you from, Ding?"

"Ding is from Taiwan."

Wilhelmina glared at me with her knuckle eyes. "I don't like to see white people speaking for brown people."

"That brown person does not know English," I said.

"Lucy is her translator," Eeyore said. "Ding only knows Formosan."

"I can speak a little English," Ding said.

Her saying this was a serious jolt to everyone, including me, but especially Eeyore, who had played dominoes with Ding for two hours silently. Renee consoled him with a punch in the arm.

"What brings you to North Carolina, Ding?" Wilhelmina said.

"*She* brings me," Ding said, nodding at me. "I go where she goes, and she will maybe just drift around and go wherever. We live a hippie lifestyle anytime."

"Thank you for speaking to us in your words," Wilhelmina said. Now she turned to me. Except for Wilhelmina, we all sat cross-legged on the ground. Wilhelmina had a pail to sit on. The daylight had dropped, and the campfire flashed on her broad, bare forehead. "Lucy, you look like jailbait," she said. "What's your story?"

"Jailbait about sums it up," I said.

"You're a runaway?"

"I suppose."

"In that case you'll be interested in what I've got to tell you," she said. "Tonight we are going to study about killing our parents."

"Heavy," Dirk said.

Eeyore said, "You don't mean really killing them, do you?"

"No, I mean something harder," Wilhelmina said. "I'm talking about killing them in your brain."

"Why would we do that?" Eeyore wanted to know.

"Because our parents made us who we are, and we don't want to be who we are anymore. Eeyore, tell this group about your parents."

"Okay. Well, my dad is a funny old gentleman. He's pretty elderly. He was forty-nine already when I was born. He knows everything about the ocean and all things maritime. Mom likes to tinkle the ivories."

"Now it's your turn, Renee," Wilhelmina said.

"He made a ship in a bottle, like with strings all over it? He's really sweet. I call him Dad, and I call Eeyore's mother Mom."

"I mean tell us about *your* parents."

"Oh. My dad is deceased, and my mom is a nurse at St. Mary's Hospital. I don't want to kill my mom."

"You don't see the need for it?"

"Not really! Do you need to kill yours?"

"No, because I already killed her, and my father, too."

"Who were they?"

"My father was an executive with the Xerox Corporation, and my mother was a schoolteacher in an all-white suburb of Rochester, New York. Both were pigs, unfortunately."

Around this point, I stood up. I couldn't take it anymore. "I see where this is going," I said, "and I would rather sleep in the woods. Come on, Ding."

I held out a hand to help Ding up and also urge her to follow, but she wouldn't look at my hand. She had her arms crossed over her chest.

"I said let's scoot, Ding! This lady is a total meathead."

Nobody spoke. Everybody was waiting to see what Ding would do. She perceived this, and it was as though I could see her slipping out from under discipline.

"That girl has oppressed me," Ding said.

"Dig it!" Dirk said.

"She will always tell me how to do something," Ding said. "Tell me how to eat. What sauce to put on food. *Don't put ketchup sauce on tomato! That is so wrong! Ding, why are you so stupid? Oh, Ding, why will you ever put ketchup sauce on that kind of food? Also you must never eat this kind of food with this utensil! Only very stupid will ever do that! Now sit this way! Ding, don't talk! Don't play radio! Now don't make hand clap!* But if that girl will almost die, probably who will take care of her? Aunt will not take care of her. Father will not take care of her! Only some stupid Chinese will ever take care so that this girl will not die. Girl, you are alive because of Chinese! Now I have said this. I want this girl to respond to my criticism."

They all looked at me.

"Look here," I said. "All of you hippies can go jump in the lake."

"Why don't you respond to that sister's criticism?" Wilhelmina said.

"Ding has exaggerated. I do not *always* tell her what to do. I did certainly tell her not to steal tuna when she could just as easily pay for it. No—excuse me. It is *even easier* to pay for the tuna."

"Why shouldn't Ding steal some tuna?" Wilhelmina said. "I steal tuna! Everybody should steal some tuna. Who is helped, when we pay for tuna?"

"The grocery store is helped," I said.

"Wrong! *The pig who owns the grocery store* is helped."

"All right. If you want to say it that way."

"Do you love bloody imperialism, Lucy?" Wilhelmina said.

"What can that possibly mean?"

Wilhelmina smiled a narrow smile at me. She wriggled her bottom against the pail seat, settling in. "Tonight we will be probing deep inside your brain, Lucy. We're going to pull some ugly things out of there and display them to you. Why don't you sit back down? Are you being made uncomfortable?"

"No."

"Anybody who needs to pee, go pee now," Dirk said. "Once we start the criticism, we won't want to pause."

Eeyore and Renee ran off in different directions.

"Is this really happening?" I said.

Nobody answered. Ding stared at the fire with her jaw stuck way out, inscrutable again.

Dirk pulled a dry cedar branch out of the woods and threw it on the fire. The flash burned some hair off his arm. When all the hippies were back in their places, Wilhelmina suggested that I respond to Ding's criticism with a self-criticism.

"All I ever did to Ding was give her money, drive her around, and feed her in restaurants," I said.

"Don't talk to us about Ding," Wilhelmina said. "We want to hear you talk about your own problem, sister."

"I'm not perfect," I said.

"Keep going."

"Ding fed me stolen tuna and dressed me in stolen clothes. I admit I have been short-tempered with her sometimes. I get cross. That's one flaw I have."

This was something in the direction Wilhelmina had in mind, but it did not go nearly far enough. What followed was a long session during which each hippie took a turn describing what was wrong with me. When I say long I do not mean minutes. I mean hours.

I will summarize.

Dirk said I had consciously or unconsciously participated in the oppression of a nonwhite sister and poisoned the air of the red cottage collective with a racist white anti-working-class mindset.

Wilhelmina said I was the property of male white America and needed to steal myself from the same. "Steal tuna, steal your body, steal the future," she said.

Renee began her turn by explaining to me the concept of revolutionary consciousness, which was the thing that was expanded when we allowed ourselves to confront one another with criticism while sitting in a circle. "Before I understood it, I felt so reluctant to confront people with my criticism!" she explained. But then she had been helped to understand it during her own criticism/self-criticism session two nights ago, after assisting Dirk and Wilhelmina in their escape from an angry farmer whose fruit they had stolen. "Isn't fruit fruit, even when it's for sale? And just like we say, 'This fruit is good,' we should also say whether this *friend* is good. So my criticism of you, Lucy, is that you really can be a little cross with Ding sometimes."

Eeyore's criticism was that he had seen me eating a meat sandwich in the drugstore, and we should not eat meat at drugstore lunch counters because it supports the meat economy. He allowed that eating stolen meat (such as stolen tuna) is all right, though, because it does not support the meat economy.

In fact, as I have already made clear, there was no meat on my sandwich, only cheese and onions. The ham was Betty's. But I did intend to eat ham and pay for it soon, so I let his criticism stand.

I let them all stand. When the session was over I thanked everyone for their observations and went off by myself to think.

could have strangled Betty. Why? I would not blame a rabid dog for frothing, nor a cyclone for turning houses over. And yet I felt surprised and hurt because the Communist whom I had been feeding and putting up in motels had suddenly begun to act like a Communist.

I recalled that hard brown ankle and how it had felt inside my fists when I was trying to pull her out of the back seat of my Scamp that time in Baltimore. How much better off I would have been, had I simply walked away from her and the Scamp both! Now I wanted nothing so much as to knock Betty down and put my elbow in her chest.

Renee found me hiding out by the well pump. The moon was bright. "I'm sorry you are sad," she said.

"I have a question for you, Renee. When I first met you and Eeyore, you were going door to door returning change. But now, according to the new line, kids don't have to pay for food anymore. Help me square it up."

She gasped and began to cry while smiling. "I never stole before we met Dirk and Wilhelmina. They talk, and nothing I say seems to make any sense! Oh, Lucy. I want there to be a new world, where all colors of people can have fun together."

"Tell me about the sleeping arrangements in this place," I said.

By the light of a candle stub she led me inside the red cottage. The floor was springy, and the air smelled like a box of old crayons. I jumped when I saw a figure sit up on the couch. It was Eeyore. He didn't speak as the candlelight slid over him.

"There is only the one sofa," Renee said. "This room is Dirk and Wilhelmina's"—she showed me a shut door—"but they don't like for others to go in."

"I guess I'll flop outside," I said.

"I wish I had a blanket to give you. I gave the towel to Ding."

We said good night.

Out by what was left of the fire, Betty had spread her towel on the ground. She slept on her side, knees and arms pulled in close. I scrutinized her face in the moonlight. The eyebrows were lifted slightly. Perhaps in her dream she was raising a pair of sticks to her mouth with a bit of pungent food pinched between the tips.

I sat staring at her from Wilhelmina's pail. At one point I touched her arm to make sure she was breathing. She shuddered and gave a long sigh.

It drove me nuts to see her lying there asleep like that. In my mind I went through twenty different ways that I might put my complaint to her in simple, clear English. *You're unfair!* If only I could speak Chinese, so I could tell her how wrong she was in words that would pierce her heart.

And then I began to marvel at myself. Was I truly sitting here on this bucket under the stars, trying to figure out how to make a mean, wiry Chinese girl *apologize to me*? Look how torn up I am, I thought—like a child in school, all because of some things this nut job has said which have *hurt my feelings*. What? That was insane. Or was it?

When I saw what she had done, I jumped off my bucket. How had I failed to see it before? The cunning Chinese had handled me right into the same position that I had handled old Henry into: coming in early, staying up late, taking foolish risks, craving approval, and generally doing everything asked in the manner of a good-hearted pet. All for someone else's benefit, namely hers! There was a term for this kind of involvement. The Chinese had me *under discipline*.

I did not walk, I ran across the yard. Ducking through a clump of trees, I breached an unusually sturdy spider's web. The threads pulled and snapped. I spun, slapping at my face, neck, and hair.

Break something else, I told myself.

I found the pair of ruts that would lead me through the hemlocks to the road. I thought I would run all the way into town. But my head was hurting again. Then I remembered the van. It would be like an Eeyore to leave the key in it.

I went back. Yes, the key was there.

68

I sat behind the wheel a moment trying to picture the way Eeyore had brought us from town. We had passed a furniture dump. That would be on my other side now, going back.

My mind went off into another place, and I sat wondering emptily.

Voices and running footsteps brought me back. I ducked to the floor as the van door slid open behind me.

There was a violent tussle in the back of the van. It seemed one person was shoving another into the van and beating him or her. I recognized Dirk's pipey voicings, though I couldn't tell which end of the beating he was on. The other voice was Wilhelmina's. They were not fighting, however. They threw their bodies against the greasy daybed at the back of the van.

Long minutes of this went by. When it was over there was a period of quiet before they spoke.

DIRK: That Renee is sweet as pie.
WILHELMINA: Mm-hm.
DIRK: I would like to lick her up one side and down the other.
WILHELMINA: Kitten.
DIRK: Not for my sake, but only for hers and that bourgeois boyfriend's. I want to smash monogamy at their house. Hand me that thing.
WILHELMINA: Here you go.

A match flared. There was silence, then the dark smell of cannabis smoke.

WILHELMINA: No, thanks. I don't want any of that right now.
DIRK: It'll make you less uptight.
WILHELMINA: Don't police me, Dirk.

DIRK: Do you see any potential in the blond kid?

WILHELMINA: I don't know. She must come from money. She has that *do-what-I-say* way about her.

DIRK: Like you do.

WILHELMINA: I can't help it.

DIRK: If she's a runaway, she'll hate her parents.

WILHELMINA: But does she hate them creatively? Or is she merely pissed off because Father won't buy her a pony? If she only hates Father because Father won't buy her a pony, then she is no use to us yet. She will have to be de-educated, then radicalized.

DIRK: Recruitable?

WILHELMINA: She's still too fat. Let her go hungry awhile, and then we can begin to vandalize her worldview.

DIRK: What about the Chinese?

WILHELMINA: I don't know. Maybe.

DIRK: I want to blow up America.

WILHELMINA: Hey, good idea.

DIRK: The stuff gets more volatile the longer it sits.

WILHELMINA: I know.

DIRK: Hit me.

Three blows followed. Dirk moaned.

WILHELMINA: I want you to sleep somewhere else tonight, kitten.

DIRK: Why?

WILHELMINA: Your fingernails are bothering me.

DIRK: You are a real white girl, you know it?

WILHELMINA: Oink. Hit me back before you go.

DIRK: I don't want to hit you right now. I feel mellow.

WILHELMINA: *Mellow?*

There was silence, then a blow, and the van door slid open and shut.

69

Wilhelmina moaned by herself on the floor of the van, and then she stopped moaning. Her nose whistled, though she kept sniffing and, from the sound of it, batting at her nose.

She began to talk again, just above a whisper. "I did it with Dirk, but I didn't let him *sleep* with me," she said. "I don't want *you* to sleep with me. I'll only sleep in groups of three or alone."

I almost answered her! *I don't want to sleep with you, either,* I almost said. But something stopped me. Wilhelmina thought she was alone. She was talking to herself, or else to a person who wasn't here.

"Sleeping in pairs is sad and bourgeois," she murmured. "If I don't get up right now, I'm going to pee on myself." She slid the door open, and I heard her scuff off.

Quietly I wormed between the seats and slipped out the door that Wilhelmina had left open. I crouched by the front of the van. There she was, not too many steps away, urinating in a square of moonlight. She held her head in both hands. When she was finished she rose a little, wagged her hips, and jogged back into the van.

I would have paid a thousand dollars for a shower right then. Instead I found some dry pine needles and rubbed them all over my arms and clothes. Then I sprinted for the road.

The stuff gets more volatile. What stuff? It did make me pause. What did they want to recruit me for?

It took me a good thirty minutes just to get down the rutted half mile between the hemlocks to where the main road was. I kept having to stop and convince myself that Dirk and Wilhelmina were only a couple of high-talking jackass hippie kids. None of their talk had meaning, because it was mainly designed to impress themselves. I'd go a little further, then I'd find myself imagining Betty in some county jail, trying to figure out what to do with a pan of cool oatmeal. Would she recognize it as food? I'd stop and spend some minutes reminding myself how sneaky and hateful Betty was. Bug out, I told myself. *No es mi problema.*

The sneakers she had stolen for me were a pretty good fit. I wished she had stolen some socks to go under them.

I wondered what would ever come of me. How long would this bug-out last? When would I see Ray? Would I ever go to college? The thought came to me that I might never see Ray again, and I put it out of my head. A more precise way to describe it is that I put the thought in a box and closed the lid. I put the box on a shelf.

I tripped on a root and wished I were in bed somewhere asleep. I got to my feet and reached the road. The walk to town would take me till daylight. I told myself, The first car that comes by, I am going to put out my thumb, and if the car doesn't slow down I will jump out in the road and wave my arms so that it *has* to slow down.

I waited a long time. A gray possum wandered into the moonlight and fumbled around on the pavement in its I'm-a-possum-please-run-over-me way.

No car came. I took the box down from its shelf and unpacked it along with some others that were there. Ray. My mother and father. Celeste and her baby named Angela. I looked closely at what was there, and I noticed what was missing. There were many things I didn't know because I had never asked Ray. Other things I wondered about that no one could ever tell me. What if my life had been different? It is the idlest question ever posed. My life was what it was.

A set of headlights approached. A pickup slowed and bent its course to spare the possum's life. I went back to the campfire and shook Betty awake.

70

"**G**ive me a cigarette," I said.

Betty sat up and rubbed her eyes. She blinked at me awhile. Then she produced a crooked half pack of Raleighs from one of her secret pockets and shook two out. She lit a match in her backward Chinese manner, swiping the book against the match head.

"Tell me how to do this," I said.

"You have never tried smoke a cigarette before?"

"I've seen it done a half a million times."

Frowning, she set the two cigarettes in her mouth and lit them both. She showed me how to take some shallow puffs to draw the smoke into my mouth. I did it awhile.

"Good enough," she said. "Now you can smoke."

The smoke made my teeth feel as though I had dried them with a paper towel. "We've got to talk," I said.

"I am here," Betty said.

I paused to collect my thoughts and arrange them. Serious lies needed telling, and for once I meant to get my lies straight ahead of time.

"First some old business," I said. "I want to offer my sincerest apology for sometimes taking a domineering tone with you. Do you know what I mean by domineering?"

"Yep."

"All right. And do you accept my apology?"

"I accept it."

"That is settled, then. Now I want you to tell me what your intentions are, regarding this country."

"Don't know what you are talking about," Betty said.

"Well, you're a Communist, correct? And you're against the U.S. So what are you going to *do* about it?"

"I would like to take a bath."

"Suppose you had the chance to strike a body blow at capitalism. For example, what if someone said to you, 'Let's go plug all the toilets at the courthouse'? Vital records are generally in the basement, so any flooding would cause a degree of mayhem."

"I don't want to cause mayhem now."

I studied her awhile. A pine cone she'd kicked onto the coals was crackling like an old record, and Betty was finishing her cigarette all the way. She always smoked them right down to the filter eventually, though it might take her a couple of sessions.

"What are you looking at?" she said.

"We are friends," I said. "Aren't we?"

"You are strange."

"I am going to give you some information that you must hold very closely. By this I mean you must not tell it to anyone, and if you do, I will deny that I said it. Understand?"

"What is it?"

"I've discovered that Dirk and Wilhelmina are political informers," I said. "They pretend to like revolution, but if they learn that you're from Red China they will surely report you to Nixon's Secret Service."

"I thought U.S. does not have political informers."

"Oh, we have them. Ours are very treacherous. Don't be surprised if one of those hippies asks you to help plan a riot soon, or place a rock on some railroad tracks, or hand out flyers. It will be a trick, you see. When they suspect someone is a Communist, they are allowed to use special methods."

"Are you lying to me?"

"No. Do you believe me?"

"If those hippies work for Nixon, I feel bad for that man."

She lay down on her towel and closed her eyes.

71

In the morning, when Renee pushed aside the front door shower curtain of the red cottage, her ears were pink, and her eyes were puffy. She wettened her hands on some dew to wash her face. Then she knelt with a pan at the fire, searing cubes of stolen Spam while Eeyore and Dirk sat watching her like patient male coyotes.

"Where is Wilhelmina?" I said.

"She likes to sleep in the van," Renee informed me sweetly.

I walked off toward the woods, as though to use the facilities.

The trick I had in mind was an old one: provoke Dirk and Wilhelmina to some mild illegal action, tip off the authorities, and get out of the way. If I could recruit Wilhelmina, Dirk would follow. Wilhelmina was a hard target, however. Where was her vulnerability? It wasn't money: her family had that, yet she lived in a shack. And it wasn't Dirk. They were intimate, but she disliked him.

I'd been chewing on the problem for a while when a better question came to me. What would *Marilyn* do in my position? I did know her work, after all. I ought to have learned something from her. How would she crack a nut like Wilhelmina? The answer: solid brass.

I went around to the van and slid the door all the way open. Wilhelmina sat up on the daybed.

"You're a pig," I said.

"What?"

"You're a G-man, a shoe. I know it. You work for the FBI!"

She pulled aside some lank, dark hair, revealing a shallow crease down the middle of her white forehead.

"What makes you think that?" Wilhelmina said.

"All this patter about my oppressing a brown sister. You've taken it straight from the handbook! I know a Hoover when I see one."

An idea crept over her face. "I think *you* are the pig," she said.

"That's right. Stolen Tuna Squad." I spat on the ground.

"You may be a narco pig! Are you waiting for us to cross the state line? Is that it? Well, we won't."

"I'm not a narco pig."

"If so, you can prove it by smoking some gage." She patted the bedding around her, looking.

"That wouldn't prove anything," I said. "A person can smoke some gage and still be a pig."

We stared at each other awhile, and then I stepped up into the van. The air was foul inside, but I slid the door shut behind me. Wilhelmina sniffed and rubbed sleep from her eyes. She didn't look so militant now. She looked like a woman who'd fallen asleep on the bus and missed her stop.

"I am not a pig," I said. "I am hiding from the pigs."

"Why are you hiding from the pigs?"

"Ding and I belong to an independent Maoist cell," I said. "We are moving like fish in the sea. Do you know what I'm saying, sister?"

It will sound grandiose, but I felt like Leopold Stokowski when I saw the color come up in her neck. I had made that happen. She must have been physically salivating, because I heard her slurp.

I fed her some details. Ding and I were just off a two-week campaign of domestic sabotage. We had poured red paint into public mailboxes all over Baltimore. "We also injected glue in stamp machines," I said. "But now the Postal Inspection Service is on our tail. Don't speak of this with Ding."

"Why not?"

"For security reasons, we never mention the action out loud. Or if we must, we refer to the action by the code word of *It*."

"*It?*"

"Right. That's the code word for the action."

"*It*," she said.

"Don't keep saying it, sister."

We went on like this until I felt pretty sure I had her on the hook. All my answers were ready. Yes, I had rioted plenty, before I quit high school to go underground. My political awakening happened on a field trip to D.C., when I heard a boy in a brown corduroy suit read a speech about

Cambodia. His motorcycle helmet had a scuff on it from a Chicago po-
liceman's billy club. Ding's criticism of me the night before was genuine;
we made it a practice to criticize each other just as often as we had the
chance.

Wilhelmina wanted to know whether Ding and I were "lesbians."

"Certainly not," I said, once I understood her meaning. "That kind of
thing doesn't serve the revolution very much."

"Is Lucy your real name?"

"No."

"What *is* your real name?"

This was one detail I didn't have ready. It seems simple enough, but in
fact it is not so easy to come up with a real-sounding name when someone is staring at you waiting. Finally I said, "I don't have a real name."

"Everybody has a name," Wilhelmina said.

"Not if you stole your own birth certificate from the courthouse and
set it on fire."

As I heard myself say this, I became depressed. Too much, too far! I
had blown the pitch.

Wilhelmina let her jaw hang until she had to drag her sleeve across
her mouth, removing the drool. "I've got to get some food," she said. She
slid the van door open and trotted off.

72

Wilhelmina eyed me fervidly across the campfire while spooning down her breakfast. Then she led me to the cottage and into the off-limits room. Dirk reclined on a mattress on the floor.

"Lucy says that she and Ding did some postal actions in Baltimore," Wilhelmina informed him.

They had me describe the actions again. "This is all new to me," Dirk said. "Are you with the Baltimore People's Front?"

"No. We are an independent cell."

"Most of the Baltimore militants report to the People's Front."

"Not us. We worked out of a hotel on St. Paul called the Fletcher."

"I know the place. It's near the Peabody Institute."

"Correct."

"You probably know the brothers in the Eager Street Collective, then."

"I'm not familiar with any collective on Eager Street."

"There's some greasers living with a lady named Mother Swink on Pratt. Bunch of tire cutters."

"I don't know any Mother Swink."

"What about the Midwives of Violence, at the University of Maryland? You must have heard of them," Dirk said.

"Nope."

"Have you heard of the University of Maryland?"

"Don't talk down to her," Wilhelmina said.

"I wasn't talking down to her. I'm trying to ascertain her place in the movement."

"You don't know every single militant in Baltimore," Wilhelmina said.

"There's some Ho-ists at Towson State." He swiveled his small eyes. "Who are you friends with?"

"You don't know much about security," I said to Dirk. "You've just described the order of battle for half of Baltimore County. If I were a pig, you'd have compromised all of them."

"Dirk, you pinhead!" Wilhelmina said.

"I don't trust her."

"I do," Wilhelmina said. "Your work pouring paint in mail slots was laudable," she said to me. "I dig that. But revolutionaries have to organize. I wonder if you're ready to take the next step."

"What step?"

"Would you fight a pig in the street?"

"Fighting pigs is no big deal. I haven't used a toothbrush in several days, so my breath could probably knock a pig over."

"Some of us are ready to get beat up or even die for the revolution," Wilhelmina said. "What do you think about that?"

"I'm in no hurry to die," I said.

Dirk gave a laugh—not even a laugh, really, but a dry blast of air from his nose. For him, apparently, dying was just a normal day at the office.

"I don't mind mixing it up," I said. I lifted my hair to show them the mark where I had run into the shovel on the front-end loader. I told them a night watchman had done it to me outside a Bank of America depository. "Ding took him out with a pipe," I said. "Then she dragged me up the alley to a candy shop."

Dirk gazed at the scabbed-over gash on my forehead with a simple, greedy awe. Both of them did. They were made stupid by it.

"I'm telling her about the action," Wilhelmina said to Dirk.

"If you tell her, she's got to become involved," Dirk said.

"Are you in?" she asked me.

"In what?" I said.

"In the action."

"I don't know what the action is."

"We can't tell you what the action is until you promise you're in."

"I'm going to have a problem with that," I said.

"I know you're not afraid," Wilhelmina said. "Do you hate the world as it is?"

"Sure I do."

"Then let's make war."

"I'm getting everyone in the van right now," Dirk said. "Bring the box." He left.

Wilhelmina gathered a few tools from the floor—a hand drill, some pliers—and set them in an Army surplus footlocker. I saw packs of flashlight batteries in there, too, along with some bundles wrapped in newspaper. Wilhelmina shut the lid and snapped a padlock.

"Grab an end, sister."

"Where are we going?"

"To the van."

The footlocker was heavy, and when I stumbled once, Wilhelmina stopped and laid a hand on her chest. "Don't drop it," she said.

The rear doors of the van stood open. We set the locker in back, behind the daybed, and covered it with some dirty canvas and a green pillowcase.

"What's that?" Renee said from on top of the bed.

"Supplies," Wilhelmina said. She climbed up to join Renee.

The engine cranked and caught. I walked around to the open sliding door. Eeyore was already at the wheel, with Dirk in the front passenger seat.

"Come on, sister!" Wilhelmina called.

"I haven't had breakfast yet," I said.

"I saved you some Spam," Renee said.

"Where is Ding?"

But there she was right in front of me, alone on the fan-backed wicker garden chair. "If I come, you come," Ding said.

I got in.

"Where are we going?" I asked.

"Washington, D.C.!" Renee said.

73

We exited North Carolina by the Blue Ridge Parkway, which runs along the top of the Blue Ridge Mountains. Betty asked for gum, but there is no place to get gum on the Blue Ridge Parkway.

"The park pigs police the parkway," Dirk said.

"I haven't seen any pigs," Renee said.

There wasn't much of anything to see—no billboards allowed on the parkway, and no Stuckey's restaurants. It was a national park in the form of a well-maintained highway. Aside from the pavement itself, the only evidence of mankind's dominion was the occasional brown speed limit sign.

Betty looked like she might cry or kill someone. I advised her to try to sleep.

The morning was long, tense, and dull. Wilhelmina explained to Renee that the park pigs were some of the basest pigs in the government, because it was their job to underestimate the size of the movement. "When a million kids stormed the Pentagon, the Park Service said there were only a hundred thousand of us."

Dirk explained to Eeyore why monogamy must be smashed. "After the revolution there will be no private property."

Betty's garden chair had one bad leg, which eventually broke off. Down she went. Wilhelmina laughed—not a pretty sound. Betty got to her feet and, very practically I thought, smashed the chair against the steel floor until the other three legs were also broken off. She then had the benefit of the comfortable wicker seat and the large, fan-shaped backrest while stretching her legs out in front of her, crossed at the ankles.

I got by with a dirty red pillow, fringed in gold at the seams.

Dirk proposed we all take our clothes off and entwine our bodies on the floor of the van.

"No," said Wilhelmina, Betty, Renee, Eeyore, and I.

His next idea was that we get off the Blue Ridge Parkway and find some gum for Ding.

"All right," Eeyore said.

We left the parkway and stopped at a Gulf station. Dirk seemed to know the attendant. They hugged and shared an elaborate handshake. When we were in the van and moving again, Dirk passed around a sack of green, apple-flavored bubble gum. Mine had a little stamp inside the wrapper, like an S&H green stamp, only smaller. We all had these stamps, except for Eeyore, who was driving.

"What are these little stamps?" Renee said.

"Lay it on your tongue. Like this," Dirk said.

She did it, and so did Wilhelmina. Now they watched Betty and me.

"It builds cadre spirit," Wilhelmina said.

"And proves you're not a pig," Dirk said.

I put the little stamp on my tongue as Dirk and Wilhelmina watched. Betty did the same.

Renee described an experience she'd had while camping with the youth group from her church. A bunch of them were holding plastic forks over the fire, causing the tines to curl. Then she put a Styrofoam cup on a stick, and a drop of molten Styrofoam landed on her fingertip. She showed us the scarred cuticle.

"Still, you have a handsome set of paws," Wilhelmina said.

All of us examined Renee's hands. The fingers were long, though not too long, and the skin had a wholesome, healthy, elastic appearance. The bluish veins branched and cornered like U.S. routes on a map.

"My old paws are awfully scaly," Wilhelmina said.

"Mm, yes," Renee said. She examined them clumsily, front and back.

"Maybe you can put some lotion on those hands," Betty said.

We took turns scrutinizing Betty's hands. They were as hard as wooden spoons.

Eeyore had the handsomest set of hands aboard. The same quality that was so unappealing in his feet, namely their expressiveness, was a virtue in his hands. He didn't carry much meat on his bones, but Eeyore's skeleton was substantial. He had big knuckles, too.

"Eeyore's hands make me sad," Renee said. She began to cry.

Dirk's hands were like possum hands. Pink, with wrinkled knuckles and pale, horny nails. His hands seemed made for reaching and scratching *up under* things, like up under dashboards, sofas, or pant legs.

"Don't cry," Eeyore said.

I was well aware that I had ingested some kind of narcotic substance with that paper stamp. I'd considered it necessary to establish good faith with these dangerous hooligans. I waited for my mind to be blown. Yet nothing much happened to me.

Renee was up front in the passenger seat holding hands with Eeyore, who still drove. Dirk had taken his clothes off and was loping in an ape-like posture in the back of the van while Wilhelmina twitched on the daybed.

I began to suspect that I had some kind of natural resistance to whatever was in the stamp.

Betty sat quietly. On the floor next to her was an animal about the size of a large tomcat. Its body and tail were covered with leathery gray scales. *A pangolin.* I hadn't seen one of those in a long time.

I asked Betty, "How do you feel?"

"I feel *different,*" she said.

"I don't."

"Everything feel so soft."

"How did that pangolin get in here?"

"I don't know what a pangolin is."

"Look, it's right there."

"Don't see it."

The pangolin stood, lifting its front legs off the floor. It was difficult to tell for sure in which direction it was looking. Its eyes were positioned on the sides of its head, like a horse's eyes. There was a nonspecific vigilance about the creature: the wariness of the grazer. The eater of insects.

"When I was a small girl," I said, "some boys brought a live pangolin to the house for us to eat. Judith gave them some money for it, but then she wouldn't cook it. She said we must never eat a pangolin. Judith was a Congolese lady. She put the dogs in the shed, and then she put the pangolin on the ground. It stood up and walked into the bush."

Betty wasn't listening. She was singing in her high, quavering Chinese singing voice.

Dirk was urging all of us to take all our clothes off and criticize Wilhelmina. I don't know what road we were on. We rolled through towns. Renee had a hand on the top button of her shirt, but she was not quite fully persuaded yet. Eeyore kept an eye on her over his shoulder as he drove. I noticed lots of flags out. I didn't think anything of it. I had forgotten what day it was.

"Go ahead and criticize me," Wilhelmina said. "Pelt me with doctrine."

From outside the van there came a noise like artillery.

Behind us in the road, six or seven ranks of girls in white tights and spangled blue leotards were marching in close formation. They carried bright rifles. They all wore snowy eye makeup, too.

Wilhelmina began to scream.

A line of cymbals flashed in the sun, and a band blasted out the "Marines' Hymn." It's a stirring tune, even if, like me, you're not sure what the halls of Montezuma are. The girls pitched their rifles over their heads, and the rifles hung spinning until the girls snatched them down.

"I do believe we are inside of a Fourth of July parade," Dirk said.

Wilhelmina squealed and wriggled, and the rest of us kept falling over whenever Eeyore tapped the brakes to keep from hitting some men who were driving little red cars. The men had fezzes on their heads. The sidewalks were bunched with people. In some cases, the small people straddled the necks of the large ones.

A couple of horses came alongside the van with policemen on their backs. Dirk began to look for his clothes.

"You threw your clothes out the window," Eeyore said.

Dirk pulled at Wilhelmina's shirt. She slapped his hands away.

Renee waved her lithe arms from the window, and some of the people waved back at her.

I was holding the pangolin in my lap through all of this, hidden underneath my hands. It had a way of rolling its body into a ball.

Eeyore got us out of the parade and found a place to park. In the back of the van he went from person to person, settling people down. Wilhelmina clenched her eyes, then woke up ready to lead the study group. "Let's all clean our buckets out!" she said.

Dirk was first. "Sometimes I can't concentrate because of my horniness," he said.

"Before I was in love with Eeyore," Renee said, "I was in love with someone else."

"I feel guilty for not going to Vietnam," Eeyore said.

Betty spoke some language while rolling her eyes, and then she punched her thigh.

"What is it?"

"I am speak Chinese with American accent," she said. She laughed and laughed.

"I once had a friendly uncle," Wilhelmina said.

"That's nice," Renee said.

"No, it isn't."

This went on for an hour or more. A lot of buckets got emptied in the van.

"Go on and clean your bucket with us, Lucy," Wilhelmina said.

"My bucket is already clean."

"If so, you are a marvel."

"Let's have a corn dog," I said.

We got out of the van and walked to where the corn dog stand was. The parade was long over, and I don't know why the stand was still open. The man was dipping corn dogs to order. They came hissing from the grease. "Corn dog is good!" Betty said. She paid for everyone.

While the others were distracted, I slipped off behind a pile of tires and set the pangolin on the ground. It unballed itself and climbed into a trash can. Perhaps the kind of food it liked was there.

The others were waiting for me in the van. I got in and we left.

It was evening when we crossed the Potomac. Traffic was slow, and Eeyore got lost. He had gotten us there alive, though. We climbed out into a thick flock of longhairs at Dupont Circle. It was raining. Dirk had on some overalls of Wilhelmina's; I saw his naked gray heels flash, and he disappeared into the crowd. Wilhelmina sank into a heap. Eeyore clung to Renee, and she petted him constantly. I heard her say into his ear, "I would never do that."

Eeyore paid some quarters so we could go under a tarp and see a thing called "The Dave Wilson Millipede Circus." In fact Dave Wilson's millipedes didn't do much but crawl over some miniature playground equipment while Dave Wilson blew songs on a harmonica. When one of the millipedes fell an inch it would coil up and be still awhile.

"It's a traveling millipede circus," Dave Wilson explained to Renee. "When I get enough quarters, I'm going to Kentucky."

"Anywhere sounds better than here," Eeyore said.

I lost Betty and then I found her again under a tree, eating peanuts from a bag.

We watched fireworks, and then we fell asleep.

Before dawn, someone waked Betty and me up and asked us if we wanted a bath. Of course we did. Ten or a dozen of us got into Dirk's van. Dirk and Wilhelmina were there. Eeyore and Renee had left, I guess. Maybe they went with Dave Wilson to Kentucky. I never did see them again.

The van stopped near the Capitol, and we walked west along the lit-up Mall. There'd been an awfully big party there the day before. The grass was chewed up and littered with trash. A few stragglers lay under blankets, or under each other. The Smithsonian Castle shone black with glitter points. We sauntered, soaking wet, some of us pausing to howl or scratch. It had rained all night, and it was raining now.

Betty touched my arm. "Where are we?"

I told her where we were.

"Something strange has happened," she said. "No more apple-flavor gum."

The two of us found a bench. Ahead of us, at the Reflecting Pool, the men and women we'd come here with were stripping off their clothes. Their figures were small and pale, the voices mild and faraway-sounding. So this was where we were to bathe. A tall fellow waded in circles in the fountain, gathering pennies into a sock.

"D.C. has a big Chinatown," Betty said. "I think I will go there."

"What about Wang? You said that he could find you in any Chinatown."

"I know how to deal with those people. I don't want to stay with these hippies anymore."

We sat awhile.

The sky over the Capitol turned pink. On the sidewalk I noticed some worms—*many* worms. Hundreds of them. The big ones were long and doughy, the small ones little more than pencil strokes. They were everywhere. At a puddle in the sidewalk a huge clot of them had massed up like a pound of fresh hamburger, striving together.

I asked Betty, "Do you see these worms?"

She got down on her haunches like a baseball catcher and cupped a worm in her hands. Her hands were pale inside. The worm flipped as though trying to right itself.

"I do see worms," Betty said.

We were studying the flipping worm when we heard screams. I wasn't too alarmed, by now. It was only some Girl Scouts, up early and hysterical. Three of them shared two umbrellas, hopping on the sidewalk, squealing and laughing, splashing in their saddle shoes. They saw the worms, too. It was an ordinary, real, post-rain earthworm rising.

Betty laid her worm on the grass. "Goodbye worm," she said.

It was at this point that I advised Betty of the truth, that I had held certain things back from her regarding my identity and associations, etc. I did not tell her what my associations were. There was simply a desire to clear the air. "I have lied to you a good deal," I said.

"I know that already."

In spite of trying not to, I began to cry. "I oppose your ideology," I said, "but I wish your Chinese people well." I told her how to get to Chinatown.

"Goodbye," she said, and she walked off the way I had told her to go, back up the Mall and past the Museum of Natural History. Beyond that she would go north until she came to H Street, where she would turn right and just keep going until she found herself surrounded by signs with Chinese writing on them. That was the last I saw of Betty.

74

The sixth of July was a Thursday. The streets had been washed, and the sky was mostly empty. In the van Wilhelmina read aloud to us about the night the Bolsheviks killed Czar Nicholas and his heirs in a basement, bunching them up as though for a family portrait, then cutting them down with guns and bayonets.

We all had new clothes on, or new old clothes, from the Salvation Army store. Wilhelmina had chosen a tailored skirt and jacket made of coarse, knobbly orange and magenta stuff. She'd found some pumps that nearly went with the suit, and up top she had on a cloche hat that covered her ears. Her calves were nicked and bloody from a public restroom shaving.

Dirk was in dark blue business attire. The suit had an off smell but looked all right.

I had on cowboy boots and a blue DuPont raincoat.

The bomb was in pieces in our clothes. Our plan was to enter the Department of the Interior building one at a time. Each of us would take the elevator to a different floor, then we'd meet in a back stairwell. Dirk would leave the assembled bomb in a men's-room stall near the offices of the National Park Service.

In the van Wilhelmina stopped reading and closed her book. The czar had gone quickly, but some of the family had lingered through long stabbings. Wilhelmina's cheeks were wet. Dirk asked her why she was crying.

"Because I'm so happy," she said.

I hoped to see her in handcuffs soon. We were to enter the building separately, five minutes apart, and I'd agreed to go in first. Once I got upstairs, all I had to do was knock on any door and ask a secretary to telephone the guard in the lobby. Wilhelmina and Dirk could be safely picked off as they entered. I would try to slip away; and if I couldn't, so be it.

The United States Interior Department faces C Street and occupies a whole block. Dirk drove all the way around the building once, looking for a parking space. "I can't walk far with this flashlight taped on my leg," he said.

Wilhelmina was breathing loudly through her mouth.

"This may be our last day to walk on the street," Dirk said. His voice reached a high note. "If we're caught, they'll put us away forever."

"We don't matter," Wilhelmina said.

"Maybe we should be doing something more important than this," Dirk said. "The Park Service is an *extremity.* We should go for the groin."

"Too late," Wilhelmina said. "We're here. We're doing this."

Dirk jerked the wheel. He turned onto Virginia Avenue.

"Turn around," I said. "Wilhelmina's right."

"Let me think!" he said.

Wilhelmina stared at him.

We passed Howard Johnson's and the Watergate. I could almost see the roof of Mrs. Edel's house on I Street.

We drove along Water Street under the elevated freeway into George-town. There was the Francis Scott Key Bridge with its arches and the Popsicle-shaped caves above them. When Water Street came to an end, Dirk turned the van around. Soon we were crossing the river.

"Where are you taking us?" Wilhelmina said.

"To the place we've always wanted to go," Dirk said.

He took a book from under his seat and handed it to her. The jacket was gray and black with orange lettering, and I knew the book immediately. It happened to be a book I had read.

75

I am talking about a book called *The Craft of Intelligence* that was written by Allen Dulles after he was sacked by President Kennedy over the Bay of Pigs. According to Miss Evans it is the book that is checked out of the Farm library more than any other. It is not the sort of book a person living an Agency cover can keep in his living room, even though there's nothing classified in it.

Wilhelmina opened it to the place that was marked: an aerial photograph of the Headquarters building in Langley. She spoke some profanities.

"We'll come in this way," Dirk said, tracing a line up her sleeve toward the picture.

"They're not going to let us walk in the front door of the CIA," Wilhelmina said.

"They *will*," he said. "We only have to get onto the grounds. Once you're on the grounds, you *can* walk in the front door. It's open."

"How do you know that?"

"I read it in *Ramparts*."

"It doesn't seem prudent," Wilhelmina said.

"Was Che prudent?"

"Che's dead."

"You're thirty-two," Dirk said. "How long do you want to live?"

With her small, square teeth Wilhelmina chewed her lips.

We rode the George Washington Parkway west of town through Fairfax County. Dirk pulled the van off at a wide spot. "Come into the woods with me," he said. We followed him. The damp ground was slick under hard soles. He brought some balls of leaves out of his black shoulder bag. They were baseball-sized. He gave one to each of us. "I got these from a Vietnamese sister yesterday," he said. "Open them."

Inside each ball was a lump of plain rice.

"This is how our brothers in the Viet Cong eat," Dirk said. "Let's eat now while we think about three million brown people who have died."

"I'm not eating this rice out of a leaf," I said.

Wilhelmina buried her mouth in it.

Dirk produced a set of bolt cutters, which he used to cut a flap in an eight-foot chain-link fence. On the other side, more woods. We slipped through in our Salvation Army suits.

"Now we'll assemble the device," Dirk said.

I reminded him we had planned to do that inside.

"There may not be time inside, Lucy. If we do it now, we can carry it in, drop it in a toilet stall, and get out the way we came."

"We'll never get out," I said.

"Let's do it," Wilhelmina said. She stripped her jacket off. She had a roll of black vinyl tape and two pencil-shaped blasting caps in the lining. "Come on, Lucy."

I dropped the raincoat. Underneath it I had on a fishing vest with five sticks of dynamite in it.

Dirk taped the sticks alongside his flashlight—a cheap one containing four batteries. He'd rigged it so some loose wires dangled from the switch. Eeyore's wind-up alarm clock went on top. Small screws had been added on the face and minute hand. Dirk wound the clock and taped it in place. His hands were steady as he pressed the two blasting caps longways into two sticks of dynamite.

"Why do you need two of those?" I said.

"One could fail." He set the crude device in his shoulder bag and presented it to Wilhelmina, who pulled the strap over her head.

Beyond a second fence, it was just as Dirk had said it would be. No security anywhere. We stepped off a curb and crossed a parking lot. Each car had its permit hanging from the rearview mirror. They were ordinary cars in an ordinary parking lot. If anything, the parking lot was duller than most. The permits had only numbers on them.

Before this day I had never been to Agency Headquarters. I had wondered about the place and studied the pictures that are available. In some you can see what looks like a wide tent or awning at one end of the Headquarters building, and I had assumed that to be the front, but I now saw it wasn't. The building they call the Bubble was at the front. It is a white, dome-shaped auditorium resembling the crown of a mushroom. We passed a few people, and no one stopped us or seemed to notice us much. One fellow, who had a bench in the sun to himself, was eating peanuts.

A part of my mind had forgotten why I was there until Dirk dropped the door on Wilhelmina's arm. She made no sound, but I saw her cringe, and when her head turned I saw her grinning.

The lobby of the Headquarters building is mostly white stone. At the center of the floor is the Agency seal, done in black granite. Two uniformed guards stood well back from the entrance. It's a bare, sterile room—no curtains to hide behind, no cubbies to tuck things into. A few plain chairs were lined up by the wall.

A woman stood with her back to us. Wilhelmina asked her where the ladies' room was.

The woman was smiling when she turned. "You'll have to wait for your escort," she said. "There's no ladies' room on this side."

Dirk went limp when a man touched his shoulder. It happened fast. That man and one other caught Dirk by the arms and led him away.

Wilhelmina saw it happen, and I watched the understanding cross her face. Here we were: we had walked right in, led by Dirk, and why? She was frozen very briefly. Then she ran, or tried to. The pumps slid out from under her. She hit the floor hard on her hip.

Men had appeared behind us to block the door. Suddenly they were everywhere. Wilhelmina scrambled to the wall, kicking her scratched legs. She got behind a chrome and vinyl chair. Men were running across the floor, soles clacking and making a rain of echoes.

Wilhelmina stuck her arms into the bag. She brought the ugly, taped-up device out onto her thighs. What a shoddy-looking thing it was—a child's first science project. The circle of men who'd been closing around us stopped. Wilhelmina pinched the hands of the clock together. She held her white thumb on the flashlight switch.

"Come closer," she said.

The only other woman in the crowd—the one who'd smiled—had my arms pinned. "All she has to do is push the switch," I told the woman.

The woman asked me whether I was afraid, and I told her I was.

"Don't be," she said in my ear. "It's only glue and sawdust."

The officers who surrounded Wilhelmina stood their ground as she cradled the toy bomb in her lap, spitting and barking profanities at them. She flung her head backward, and I heard it knock the marble—a loud, sickening sound. She did it again.

No one here was afraid of Wilhelmina's bomb. The only thing these men were wary of was the hysterical woman on the floor. She could bite, scratch, and kick with her heels. She was hopeless and had her shoulders to the wall.

"Settle down, Louise," someone said to her.

That was another surprise for me. Louise Larch is now a household name, but in the short time I knew her, I never once heard her called that.

She screamed and threw her head against the stone again.

"*Ouch*," an officer said. Some people laughed.

I tried to pull my arms free. "Someone stop her," I said.

No one moved. Louise Larch slung her head against the wall again. She screamed this time. It was too much. I raised my leg and dragged it down the inside calf of the woman who had my arms, planting my boot sole hard on her arch. She let go. I ran at Wilhelmina and grabbed her head to drag her away from the wall.

She bit me hard between my thumb and first finger. She got a good hold of me with her little square teeth and wouldn't let go. I howled. Then she pushed the flashlight switch, and both of us got a surprise. Louise Larch had thought we were going to die, I guess. And I'd thought nothing would happen. Wrong again.

I only wish the genius who gave Dirk that fake dynamite had also thought to give him some fake blasting caps.

People at my new school are always asking me how I got my glass eye. I tell them I was born with it. Some of these West Virginia kids are not as dumb as they look, however. In the high school parking lot I saw a boy weld two bumpers together using a car battery and a set of jumper cables. Everyone had a laugh except for Mr. Breen and Miss Bowers, whose bumpers they were. I'm not driving cars anymore until I'm legal. Mrs. Gandy drops me off and picks me up in her long, tan Chrysler.

Since I moved in with the Gandys she has been kind enough to lay off of the prying questions. I know she is curious about my early life. So am I, sometimes. Had we reconverged, I would have had many things to talk about with Ray.

Mr. Gandy turns into a storyteller when he has had a few drinks. I asked him one night to tell me why, in 1960, Ray went to Stanleyville. What was the intelligence requirement?

"I don't remember precisely, Angela. It had been an important city under Belgian rule. We were there because we were everywhere. The truth is, I never understood that place nor knew what the hell was going to happen next. Africa! Stanleyville had a university, but it fell to forty witch doctors walking down Main Street waving palm leaves. The city succumbed to magic, then it ate itself. I understand the Soviets, and I am beginning to make some sense of the GOP, but four years in the Congo left me none the wiser. We must have done something right, however, because the Republic of Zaire remains a staunch ally of the Western democracies. This can only redound to its advantage in years to come."

He has offered to contact the Belgian Embassy regarding any relatives I may have. I only need to tell him what my name is. But I don't think I will.

After everything that's happened, I may as well stay Angela.

About Ray. He wasn't perfect. We were swindled on those Tennessee driver's licenses. Recently, I found out that the real ones don't even have photos. It is a little yellow card with typing on it. Also, Marilyn was right that we should have had a better system of communication set up for after the bugout. I understand the *World News Digest* with my "all clear" in it was lying under the mail slot when Mrs. Edel and the meter reader found Ray.

I don't know why he went back to I Street. He told me not to go there. It was the last place I'd have looked for him. Maybe he didn't know how sick he was, or maybe he did know. The coroner's certificate says his death was from "acute alcohol withdrawal."

If he were alive he would be in jail now with HORSEFLY and GRISTLE and the rest of them. GRISTLE: he thought Watergate might hurt Nixon. But he gave the people of this country too little credit. The voters have once again decided for themselves, and as I write this the President is about to begin his second term. A year from now, I imagine the break-in will mostly have been forgotten, except by the few whose lives were wrecked by it.

I think Ray would not have minded jail so much, but seeing his face in the paper would have been a terrible thing. He was one of the men who worked quietly, content to have his medal locked away in a safe in Langley. I loved Ray because he pulled me down from a tree on the day I lost everything, and I regret that I wasn't with him in the end. He died downstairs on the couch without a blanket. Evidently he was too ill or not thinking straight enough to get upstairs to where the blankets were. I could have helped with things like that and would have done so bravely, though I suspect he didn't want me to see him die. The first thing Ray ever said to me was "Don't be scared," and I'm not and I would have liked to return the kindness.

One final thing.

I don't know where Betty or "Ding" is, and asking me a thousand times won't change it. The last time I saw her was the fifth of July on the National Mall, when worms were creeping over the sidewalks trying not to drown. Check the weather reports. Off she went, toward Chinatown. I don't know whether she got there. I stopped looking, and she may have gone straight, right, or left. The person you are looking for is a Chinese female, five-foot-two, wiry, dark of complexion, with an overall surly, obstinate, and independent manner. There's your description. It occurs to me now she must have made a poor Maoist, back at home, considering how mulish she is, and always averse to going along with the group in even the most trivial thing.

Like they say of a mule, she would live twenty years just to kick you.

She has a few freckles across both cheeks. That's a little unusual for a Chinese, as far as I know.

The best bet for picking her up will be on a shoplifting charge.

Your Mr. Wicker, the polygraph man, implied that I might be still in touch with Betty or even hiding her. On that subject, here are some thoughts that I hope you will consider.

Why would I want to help her in any way? She only gave me headaches.

She steals, which I do not approve of except when it is necessary.

She is a Communist, which I never approve of.

Where am I going to hide a Chinese Communist in Wigmore, West Virginia? In the Gandys' spare bedroom? Mrs. Gandy would certainly notice on one of her tidying jags. In the barn? But Betty dislikes horses and she is afraid of cats.

Let me put it this way. Suppose for the sake of argument that your Mr. Wicker were correct, and I did in fact have Betty hidden away in a cave somewhere on the property, living in high style off chicken and rice and perfecting her English by reading old copies of *American Girl* magazine. In the scheme of things, so what? She is a small and insignificant person, a blip of humanity, as am I. I am not saying it is so (in fact, I am saying it is *not* so), but even if you think that such a relationship exists, why waste your time on it? It is a two-headed frog of a thing—a totally meaningless accident of nature. Nature is strange. Sometimes a horse and a goat are friends, and it is merely something weird they do. I don't know why they do it. Some horses do not get along with other horses, and some goats can get along with anything. What I am describing now is not the case, but if it were the case it would not be hurting anyone, and the best thing that you could do would be to leave it alone.

Sincerely,
Angela Sloan

Angela Sloan

A Novel

James Whorton, Jr.

Reading Group Guide

Author Q&A

ABOUT THIS GUIDE

The following reading group guide is intended to help you find interesting and rewarding approaches to your reading of *Angela Sloan*. We hope this enhances your enjoyment and appreciation of the book. For a complete listing of reading group guides from Simon and Schuster, visit www.community.simonandschuster.com/.

Angela Sloan
Reading Group Guide

Introduction

It's the summer of 1972 and one "strange, dry girl"—fourteen-year-old Angela Sloan—is on the run from the CIA, even though she is *quite* certain that her father, ex-agent Ray Sloan, had *very* little involvement in the Watergate fiasco. As Ray and Angela hit the road, sometimes together, more often apart, Angela, who prides herself on her ability to go unnoticed, finds herself in the company of rather unlikely car-fellows, such as a strange, pro-communist Chinese girl named Betty, and a bevy of not-so-laid-back hippies with their own hidden agenda. As she tries to dodge agents and find a way to reunite with Ray, Angela learns how to drive a car, smoke a cigarette, subsist on diner food, and charm a motel desk-keeper into giving her vital information; but most important, she comes to find that things are not always what they seem in this hilarious and poignant comedy of broken girls, stoic men, and mean hippies set amid the chaos of the Nixon era.

Topics and Questions for Discussion

1. Names are transient throughout the novel; many characters have more than one name, some have no real name at all, and we never do find out Angela's real name—yet, the title of the book is simply *Angela Sloan*. Discuss the significance in relation to the story and Angela's journey.

2. Angela experiences a significant journey through the course of the novel, both literally and emotionally. Compare the early version of Angela with the girl she is by the end. Do you feel she has changed? In what ways?

3. Though Angela has been raised learning all of Ray's tactics and maneuvers for reading people and scouting a situation, it is Betty who often makes the most astute observations about the people around them. For example, on page 163 she observes about Marilyn: "Way she smoke and eat, seem like she hate herself." and Angela responds, "I don't know how you could tell something like that after eating breakfast with her one time." Why do you think Betty is able to do this? Is it simply because she is more emotionally removed from the

situation than Angela is? Or do you think, in trying so hard to see everything, Angela sometimes misses the obvious?

4. Angela is horrified to discover that Betty has her, as she terms it, "under discipline," when all along she felt as though she were the one in control of the situation. Power, and the balance of power, plays an important role in every relationship throughout the novel. Discuss how each character, at one point or another, manipulates or uses their power in an attempt to achieve a particular end. In your opinion, do many of them succeed?

5. How does the relationship between Angela and Betty evolve over the course of the novel? What are the major turning points? Did you find these changes believable? Why or why not? What about the relationship between Angela and Ray?

6. Choose one adjective you think best sums up the character of Angela and share it with the group. Were you surprised by how others in your group perceived her? What are her strengths and her weaknesses? How does your perception of Angela's character change throughout the story?

7. Discuss the ways in which the bonds of family and friendship—for good and for ill—are central to the novel. Why do you think Whorton, Jr. introduces this element into the story?

8. Betty says, "You will never fool somebody with sense, but most people don't have any sense. You will be surprise. That is how I live, by so many people don't have sense." (p. 101), and Angela observes, "People look past me because I have no value to them." (p. 166) Throughout the novel, the idea that people see and believe what they wish to is repeated often. Do you agree with that concept? Why or why not?

9. The theme of appearance (versus reality) is central to the book. What are some of the obvious (and not so obvious) examples of this idea throughout the story? What do you think Angela comes to understand about the way things appear versus the way they truly are?

10. Renee and Eeyore are two characters who coincidentally pop up several times on Angela's trip, before disappearing entirely. Did you think they were working with the CIA and with Marilyn? Or that they were, in fact, just a couple of freewheeling hippies with impeccable timing? What roles do coincidence and fate play in Angela's journey?

11. While in many ways Ray trusted Angela with much more information and responsibility than most adults offer their children, he still hid a

very important secret from her about his past and his family. Do you feel he was right to keep this from Angela, or do you think by trying to protect her in this way, he ultimately did her a greater disservice?

12. Were you surprised by how Angela's adventure turned out? Why or why not?

Enhance Your Book Club

1. Read one of James Whorton, Jr.'s previous books (*Frankland, Approximately Heaven*), or another novel that shares a sassy heroine and themes of adventure and self-discovery, such as *The Spellman Files* by Lisa Lutz. How are they similar? How are they different?

2. If *Angela Sloan* was made into a movie, who would you cast for Angela? For Betty? For Ray? Discuss your Hollywood picks with you book group!

3. Do some research on the real Watergate scandal, and the tumultuous time period Angela was living in. Have each member present a fact or interesting piece of information for an impromptu history lesson! For a more in-depth account, read a book like *All the President's Men* by journalists Carl Bernstein and Bob Woodward, and discuss.

A Conversation with James Whorton, Jr.

1. This is such a hilarious, zany, offbeat adventure—where did the idea for *Angela Sloan* first come from? Was the story inspired by research on Watergate and the time period, or was it a certain character or setting that sparked the entire novel?

My daughter was home with a cold, and we spent a day watching C-Span. She was about three at the time. Alexander Butterfield was on there, telling about the moment when he revealed the existence of Nixon's secret taping system. It was a wonderful moment, because very few people knew about the tapes. A Congressional staffer just happened to ask him, hey, you guys didn't tape every word of every conversation in the Oval Office, did you? Why yes, we did. That's what got me thinking about Watergate again.

Then there was also a separate idea about a girl who is traveling the country without her father, sending him messages. I don't know where that one came from.

2. It's one thing to build a novel around a relatively unknown event in history, but quite another to take perhaps the greatest political scandal in the U.S. and give it such a twist! How did you decide to tackle this time period in this tongue-in-cheek fashion?

Well, a lot of strange things happened. It's hard to tell it straight. I think I left some of the crazier parts out, just for the sake of maintaining the very minimal standard of plausibility that I do try to maintain. For example, I left out the Cubans who were hired to shout "traitor" at Donald Sutherland. Nixon did that, or his people did. But it sounds kind of made-up, I think.

Same thing with the Congo interventions. It seems like a stretch to have Che Guevara organizing French lessons for the Congolese, but that happened. He was there, doing that. It's also true that the CIA had a plot to kill Patrice Lumumba, the first elected leader of the Congo, by poisoning his toothpaste. But I didn't put that in, because I don't know what to do with it. Do you laugh, or do you howl? It's not just bad, it's like wax museum land. Too scary, too circus-nightmare. Howard Hunt in a red wig. Sorry, no. The world inside a novel is less than real, but the advantage to this is that you can imagine it. It's a step toward imagining reality, though it doesn't get you quite there.

3. This is your third book. Was the process or experience of writing *Angela Sloan* different in any way from your previous two novels? Do you have a favorite and least favorite part of the writing process?

This one was much slower. Slow, slow. I did a lot of reading and studying, and some traveling, and I enjoyed that a lot, though it took time. I visited the CIA, and I went back to Baltimore, where I lived for a while, to remember what that was like. I walked all over DC. There was also the complication that Angela is very different from me. To begin with, she's a girl. Most of the important characters in this book are women. The men are the opaque ones, which is backwards from how a novel by a man usually works, I think.

4. There are great descriptions of how to read and react to people in the novel, such as Ray's tutorial on getting someone "under discipline"

in the motel. Were these lessons based on your own observations of human behavior?

In that case, no—the tutorial that Ray gives Angela is the method that is really taught and used by case officers in the clandestine service. I first read about it in a book by Miles Copeland called *Without Cloak or Dagger*, but it's described elsewhere, too.

5. Many authors find that their characters are extensions of themselves, in one way or another. Do you find that to be true? Which character do you identify with most? Are any of the characters in *Angela Sloan* based on people you know?

They're all based on people I know, but in piecemeal ways. None is based on a single person. I don't really think they're extensions of me. I guess the one I identify with most is Ray, though the book does not really delve into him much. He's there, but he's not very articulate.

6. The concept of names, and their importance (or lack thereof), is an interesting one—how did you name your characters? Was it random, or was there a process involved? Do any of the names or code names have a deeper significance than would appear on the surface?

I don't think too much about the names—something comes up, and maybe it seems right, and then it sticks. I tried to avoid loading the code names with too much significance. Richard Helms, who was Director of Central Intelligence during Watergate, said he used to keep a list of random words, and when they needed a new code name they would take the next one on the list. This was supposed to keep them from accidentally choosing a word that would signify something. Sometimes the names were suggestive anyway, though. For example when Lyndon Johnson had the CIA investigate the antiwar movement, which of course was something they should not have been doing, that program was called CHAOS.

7. From D.C. to Baltimore to West Virginia, Angela's forced road trip takes her to a whole host of places. Are any of the locations she ends up passing through inspired by your favorite destinations?

Yes. They are all places I've lived or spent time in and have lots of affection for. The interstate bridge over the Holston River—I lived about four miles from there.

8. What do you hope readers will take away from Angela's story?

I hope people will be entertained. Also, give an old man a break sometime.

9. Your bio notes you are both a "former Mississippian" and a "former Tennessean," and you now live in New York. How does your background inform your writing?

I wonder about that. I don't know. I do think people are different, in different places. Angela's not really from anywhere, and I sort of know that feeling.

10. Who are your writing influences? What are you currently reading?

Well, I met a Congolese English professor by email and asked him to recommend something, and he recommended *King Leopold's Ghost* by Adam Hochschild. So I'm reading that. And I just finished a book by Chris Lear called *Running with the Buffaloes* about the University of Colorado cross country team of 1998, and before that a novel by my fellow Hattiesburger Elliott Chaze called *Black Wings Has My Angel*, and before that a really good novel by Diane Johnson called *The Shadow Knows*. And I got Thomas Powers's new book *The Killing of Crazy Horse*, which I am looking forward to. He wrote maybe the best book ever on the CIA, *The Man Who Kept the Secrets*. Another one by him that's worth reading is a book called *Diana: The Making of a Terrorist*. It's about Diana Oughton, who was with the Weather Underground.

11. Now that Angela's story is complete, what's next for you?

Something fast. And something set in Rochester, I think. I'm still kind of new here and trying to get a grasp of the place. It's a city, yet there are deer and turkeys everywhere. And we occasionally see black squirrels, which I would not have believed, had I not seen them.

About the Author

James Whorton, Jr. is the author of two other novels, *Approximately Heaven* and *Frankland*. A former Mississippian and former Tennessean, he lives in Rochester, New York, with his wife and their daughter. He teaches at SUNY Brockport.

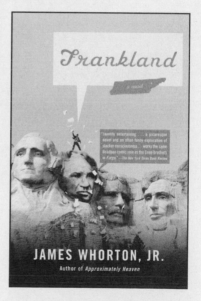